7: FEN'S REVENGE

"Where's Danny then?" were Mum's first words when she opened the door. It was ten o'clock and I'd had to ring the bell. Mum was sounding suspicious and I wasn't surprised.

"There's something on TV he wanted to get back for, so I said I was fine for the last few metres."

"Oh," was all Mum said to that. I called out "Night," to Dad, then went upstairs wearily, and plonked down on my bed staring into space, deep in thought. It was no good, I couldn't keep this up. I did a quick tot up of how many lies, however small, I'd had to tell in just one evening. I hated telling lies. Worse than that, I hated myself when I told lies.

I lay awake for ages that night, because it's difficult to sleep when you hate yourself.

Also in the Café Club series by Ann Bryant

The CAFE Club

7: FEN'S REVENGE

Ann Bryant

Hippo

Scholastic Children's Books,
Commonwealth House, 1–19 New Oxford Street,
London WC1A 1NU, UK
a division of Scholastic Ltd
London ~ New York ~ Toronto ~ Sydney ~ Auckland

First published by Scholastic Ltd, 1996

Copyright © Ann Bryant, 1996

ISBN 0 590 13887 1

Typeset by TW Typesetting, Midsomer Norton, Avon

Printed by Cox & Wyman Ltd, Reading, Berks.

*With grateful thanks to
Sheila Hume, Val Chantler
and Antony Hinge for all their help.*

Chapter 1

Hi! It's me, Fen. I'm the ambitious one, and right now I'm regretting it, because one of my great ambitious ideas seems to be going completely and utterly wrong. In fact, I'm in the kind of mess that usually reserves itself in life for Luce.

"Hang on, Fen…" (I've taken to talking to myself these days, which Tash says is the first sign of madness.) I've just realized I haven't explained about me and my five really good friends.

We're all thirteen. We all live in a small town called Cableden and we all go to Cableden Comp. The other thing we all do is work in my aunt Jan's café, which is in Cableden High Street. It's the most brilliant place to work and we know we're very lucky… (Except that I don't feel particularly lucky right now, but I'll come to that in a moment.) First let me describe all my friends, starting with Luce as I've already mentioned her.

Luce is short for Lucy Edmunson and she is the crazy one! She has a mass of strawberry-blonde curls, bright green eyes, a very cheeky grin and a huge talent for getting into ridiculous situations. She lives with her mum, her step-father and her eight-year-old twin brothers, Tim and Leo, who are actually only half-brothers.

Luce's best friend is Jaimini Riva and she's the brainy one. You pronounce Jaimini, Jay-m-nee, though we sometimes shorten her name to Jaimes. She is very dark-skinned because her father is black and her mother is white. She's also got lovely dark eyes and long black hair. Jaimini is an only child, but will soon be getting a little brother or sister, because her mum is pregnant.

I've got two sisters, by the way. Rachel is nine years old and Emmy is five. I may as well mention here that my hair is shoulder-length and sort of mousey brown – definitely nothing to kill for – and I'm quite thin and ordinary-looking. Luce says she'd love to have a face like mine because I've got prominent cheekbones!

My best friend Tash gets cross when I say I look ordinary. She insists that my face has got loads of what she calls "character", but I reckon she's just being kind. Tash, or Natasha Johnston, to give her her full name, is the kindest, sweetest one of us all. We call her the peacemaker. She's got thick, dark hair, which is layered and thins out towards her shoulders, very dark eyes and eyebrows, but not particularly dark skin.

She has also got epilepsy, but I'm the only one of us five who knows that, because Tash worries about other people knowing. I found out by mistake, although Tash is glad I know now, because it means I can help protect her in a way. Tash lives with her mum, her fifteen-year-old brother, Danny, and her little sister Peta, who's just three and is very funny. Their parents divorced when Peta was only a baby.

Leah Bryan is the musician. She's really talented, but so modest about it. Leah plays the violin and the piano to a very high standard. She's also lovely looking with very long, pale-blonde hair and a fragile-looking face. She worries about everything, Leah does, and when she hasn't got anything to worry about, she worries about that too!

Her best friend is Andy Sorrell, the daring one. Andy's real name is Agnès, which is a French name that you pronounce Ann-yes. This is because her mother is French, which makes Andy half French. She's got a little brother, Sebastien, who's only one. Andy's dad, who most of the rest of us, *and* Andy herself, find very scary, works in

France, (even though he's English), so he's away a lot of the time.

Apart from her dad, nothing scares Andy, which is why we call her the daring one. For example, if Leah left her violin in the middle of a field one day, and the next day the field was full of bulls, I do believe Andy would face the field of bulls and rescue the violin for Leah. This is even more amazing because Andy is the smallest of us all, with cropped, dark hair, big brown eyes and the darkest skin after Jaimini.

Right now, I thought, as I sat at our kitchen table daydreaming, Andy will be just starting work at the café. It was a Wednesday evening and the time was six-thirty.

Let me explain about the café. The six of us all take turns to work there one day each after school from four till six, and then the sixth person does Saturday from two-thirty to six-thirty. We have a rota so that everybody gets to do a Saturday, which, of course, is the favourite day to work as you get more pay.

We'd been ticking along like that, quite happily – apart from the odd upset (!) – when Yours Truly here had this brilliant brainwave of trying to get more business for the café by opening up one evening per week. My aunt Jan thought this was a great idea, and actually set it in motion, opening the café every Wednesday evening.

Jan – (I dropped the "aunt" bit a long time ago) – is forty-one, slim, fit and divorced. I have the slight suspicion that the reason she was so struck on my idea about opening in the evening was because she was keen to attract a different type of customer, including maybe a few single men!

So far we've had two Wednesday evenings. I was lucky and worked the very first one, along with Jan, of course. Tash did the second one, and tonight it's Andy's turn. None of our parents mind because it's only one evening every six weeks, which is hardly noticeable.

That first Wednesday that I worked proved my theory about Jan is right, because sure enough, quite a few men dropped in for a quick drink on their way home from work. It's true that there were also quite a few women who called in on their way home from work too, but I reckoned Jan was keeping her eyes open in case a nice, tall, dark, single man happened to pop by one Wednesday evening!

Jan has had quite a few boyfriends or men-friends, or whatever you call them, since her divorce, which was years ago. Somehow, though, none of these relationships has ever worked out. Anyway, to get back to the present, or rather, to the present *problem*…

I was sitting at the kitchen table, thinking about Andy at the café, when I suddenly remembered something that Tash had told me, with great concern, the previous Wednesday evening. She'd been absolutely convinced that someone was watching her, and she'd finished up by getting paranoid about it, confiding in me the next day that this man might have noticed that she'd got epilepsy, and was going to report her or something.

Poor Tash. I calmed her down and told her that that was quite impossible because Tash hardly ever has any fits these days, now she's got the right tablets to control them. And anyway, her fits aren't bad. What Tash has got is called *petit mal*, and the fits are actually called absences. All that happens when Tash has an absence is that, for anything from ten seconds to about two minutes, she sort of switches off completely. It's almost as though she's gone to sleep very fleetingly, except that she doesn't close her eyes. Her eyes go dreamy, and her eyelids might drop a little, and her face twitches, especially round her mouth. The trouble was that if her epilepsy had been any worse than this, like if she had fits very regularly or she actually fell down during a fit, then she wouldn't be allowed to work at the café.

I don't know why I'd suddenly started thinking about that just then, when the conversation was almost a week old, but I did, and as I did, an awful realization hit me. It was obvious to me that this man hadn't been staring at Tash because he guessed she was epileptic. So if he *hadn't* been staring at her for that reason, then why *had* he been staring?

The answer jumped out at me. *Because he thought she was under age to be working so late!* Yes! That was it! *Omigod!* You may wonder why that thought was so shocking. I'll tell you why. Because, if that *was* what the man was wondering, he was absolutely right. And it was all *my* fault!

You see, I'd been so totally rapt about the brilliant idea of opening the café once a week in the evening, and so proud that I'd been the one to think of it, that when the question of us six being too young to work after seven o'clock in the evening came up, I stupidly told a couple of lies to get round the problem.

It's not like me to tell lies, except white ones, and I really despise people who aren't truthful, but my first lie just popped out before I could stop it, and once it was out there was no going back.

This first lie that I told was to Jan. When she pointed out that there may be a law against girls under a certain age working in the evening, I said, "No honestly, Jan, it'll be OK because Mum's already contacted the LEA and they said there was no problem as the work was on such an infrequent basis. They said it wasn't regular

7

enough to be called a job – um – as long as you're there on the premises too, of course…"

I had said all this very glibly and I'll never know if it was because Jan was on a high about the whole idea or what, but she'd accepted every word I'd said without question.

My second lie was when I was telling Mum that the Wednesday evening plan was about to be put into action. I was explaining to her that Jan was in full agreement and that I could start the very next Wednesday evening. I was to be the first one of us to work an evening session!

Mum had said, "Hold on a sec, Fen. We'd better find out how the law stands on girls of your age working in the evenings." And I had said, "No, it isn't a problem, Mum. Honestly. You see, Jan phoned up the LEA to check what the rules were, and they said that as it was only once every six weeks, it could be overlooked." Once again my lie had been totally believed, and right now I had that awful feeling that I was going to regret it – and how!

"Where are you going in such a rush?" Mum asked, as I sprang up from the table and headed for the door.

"Just remembered we've got geography home-work and Tash took the textbook home. I'm going to phone her and find out what we're supposed to be doing."

Dad eyed me briefly before turning back to the letter he was reading. Rachel and Emmy didn't even register that I'd spoken. They were glued to the television. We've only just got the TV in the kitchen, and it's proving extremely popular, except with Mum, who purses her lips and turns the volume down every time she goes past it, until it's almost impossible to hear it at all.

I legged it upstairs and into my room, clutching the phone which I'd grabbed from the sitting room, then sat on my bed and tapped in Tash's number, hoping that her little sister Peta wouldn't answer because it always took so long to persuade Peta to go and get Tash. She's such an infuriating chatterbox, Peta is.

There were three rings then nothing, so the phone had obviously been picked up, because Tash didn't have an answerphone.

"Hello," I said, after a few more seconds of silence. "Is that you, Peta?" Still there was silence. We all know Peta's really cute and all that, but believe me I could have happily throttled her at that moment. "Peta, it's Fen here. Could you get Tash, please?"

Still the silence persisted, and I began to feel alarmed. What if Tash herself had answered the phone, and she couldn't speak because she was having an absence at that very moment?

"Tash?"

I was on the point of putting the phone down and rushing round to Tash's house, when I heard the smallest of sounds. I wasn't mistaken. It was a giggle – a three-year-old's exasperating giggle.

"Peta! Look! Will you stop being such a silly girl and go and get Tash for me! This is very important."

" 'Snot as important as what I am, 'cos I am the Queen, what is the most important person in the whole wide world. So there!"

All this came out in the same breath and it was very tempting to laugh because Peta sounded so funny. However, my worry about the café soon resurfaced, making my desire to laugh fade away.

"If you don't get Tash before I count to five, the next time I see your mummy I'll tell her what a naughty girl you've been, and she won't let you watch any television or videos for a very long time. OK?"

Then I had to block my ears because Peta was bellowing to Tash at the top of her voice, but she obviously hadn't turned away from the phone. "Tasha, there's a big fat pig on the phone who wants to talk to you, what is called Fenny Penny Pig."

This time I did laugh but I covered the mouthpiece. You're probably thinking what a horrible little child Peta is, but she isn't really. Usually she's very sweet, but like all little children she has her moments!

"Hi, Fen. Sorry. Has she been awful? I was in Danny's room. I didn't even hear the phone ring."

"Never mind that, Tash. I've been thinking about that man you said was watching you all the time last Wednesday at the café. And a horrible thought has just struck me…"

"What?"

"I think he might be some sort of inspector or something. You know, checking up that everything's as it should be at the café. And maybe he thought you were under sixteen."

"But I *am* under sixteen."

"Exactly. Under age!"

"Under age for what?" screeched Tash.

"For … working late…"

I'd reached the worst part of the conversation. This was where I had to confess to Tash that I'd told the odd lie to make sure we got the jobs.

"I thought Jan said everything was fine," Tash went on. "She did. I remember. She said the education authority had no objection to our working late when it was only once every six weeks for each of us."

"The thing is, Tash, I'm afraid it was me who told Jan that. I told her that Mum had phoned the education authority, and that they said it was fine... Then I told Mum that Jan had phoned them and they said everything was fine."

"Fen, you didn't! You... Oh, Fen! Oh, no! What a mess."

In that stuttering helpless cluster of words Tash had summed up exactly what I was feeling. I braced myself because I knew I mustn't let the fight go out of me. We could get out of this somehow. We *had* to. The question was, should we go deeper into the lie, or should we pull out right there and then?

If only we all asked ourselves this very question every time we were in this sort of position. But of course we don't, do we? We just go bulldozing on, making things worse and worse.

"Tash, we've got to go down to the café right now. If that man who was watching you is there again tonight, watching Andy, we'll know I'm right. Then we've got to get Andy out before the man says anything to Jan. After all, Andy looks about eleven sometimes, she's so small."

"But if we get Andy out, who's going in? We can't leave Jan with no help."

"I'm going in," I answered, firmly.

"You? But you don't look any older than me!"

"But I can when I try," I countered. "Anyway, it's my fault, so it's only fair that I put myself in the firing line."

"Um... I suppose so," Tash agreed, doubtfully.

"I'll meet you in fifteen to twenty minutes outside the café."

"OK. See you."

As soon as I'd rung off from Tash I tapped in the café number.

"Good evening. *The Café*."

"Hi, Jan. It's me, Fen. I'm sorry to disturb you, but could I have a very quick word with Andy, please?"

"I'll just get her. Two seconds, pet."

Jan often called me "pet". It was her special word for people she liked. It was actually about ten seconds later when Andy's surprised-sounding voice came on the line.

"Fen? Is everything OK?"

"Yeah, don't worry."

Andy was only worrying because her dad didn't like her working at the café. In fact, for quite a long time he didn't know about it at all and we had one or two hairy moments trying to keep him in the dark. He knows now, although I don't think Andy's confessed about the evenings yet.

"I was just wondering," I went on. "Is there a man in the café?"

"At a rough estimate there are about six men..."

"No, I mean, has anyone been staring at you?"

"I haven't noticed, but then I've hardly been

13

out of the kitchen since I've been here. What's all this about anyway, Fen?"

"I'll explain tomorrow. The thing is, it's essential that I take over from you tonight, or we could all be in major trouble. Just stay in the kitchen as much as you possibly can until I get there, all right?"

"What are you talking about, Fen? I'm not…"

There was a long pause.

"Andy, are you there?"

"Jan's gesticulating wildly at me. I'd better go."

"See you in fifteen minutes."

"You're mad, Fen."

"See you."

"Totally mad."

It was no wonder Andy thought I'd lost one of my tiles, I thought, as I went over the conversation in my head, while applying eyeliner and mascara. I then backcombed my hair and sprayed it with hairspray until it felt like candyfloss.

We always wore our school uniform when we worked after school at the café, and on Saturday afternoons we were supposed to wear something smart and black and white, or just black if we wanted. But on Wednesday evenings, Jan had said that as long as we looked smart we could wear what we wanted. I had put on a short suede skirt with opaque tights and a tight top.

"Too tarty by a mile," observed Rachel, as I

emerged from the bedroom. Because of having an older sister whose friends are often around, Rachel is very precocious, although she does have another side to her character which is very sweet and naïve.

"It's for a reason," I told her, "but don't tell Mum. And listen, Rachel, at quarter to nine the phone will ring. It'll only ring once so don't bother to answer it. But *do* make sure you've got the phone in your room when you go to bed. Then after a minute or so, call down to Mum that I just phoned from Tash's to say that I'd be back by ten because Tash and I were doing the geography homework together as it was really difficult. Say that Danny's going to walk me back… Got all that?"

I was speaking very quickly and urgently, and Rachel's eyes were growing bigger as I talked. She realized instantly that all this was a lie, and was probably weighing up in what way she could put this unexpected bit of bargaining power to good use – something like, "I'll do that for you, Fen, if you let me wear your new top for the next two weekends."

"I'll give you a pound if you manage to say what I told you to say so that Mum and Dad don't suspect anything, all right?" I quickly offered before Rachel could come up with a condition that I didn't want to meet.

"Are you going to the café really?" she breathed in a mixture of admiration and fear. I put a finger to my lips, nodded and rushed off, looking at my watch.

"Got to go to Tash's, Mum," I flung over my shoulder, as I slipped out of the front door. "Won't be long." Then without waiting for an answer I shut the door and ran for my life. I'd already used up nearly ten minutes and I'd have to go flat out to get to the café before the twenty minutes was up.

The only times I slowed to a jog on that journey were whenever a car passed me, because I didn't want anyone driving past to stop and ask if someone was chasing me or something. At least this'll be good training for Saturday, I told myself as I worked on my breathing.

On Saturday I was competing in a cross-country event. There were eight of us in our school team but Andy and I were the only two year eights. The other girls were all year nines. I felt very honoured to have been picked because it's only quite recently that I've got so much stronger at running.

I slowed down because a dark red, familiar-looking Vauxhall was passing me. I got a good look at the driver and he got a good look at me, too. It was Mr Blundell, one of the tech teachers at our school. He gave me a strange sort of a smile

16

but then sped up again, thank goodness, and drove away.

It was certainly unfortunate that a teacher had seen me, because this might raise questions at school, and the fewer people who knew about the evening sessions at the café, the better.

Actually, there was one other time that I slowed down and that was because a really nice-looking boy was approaching me. The nearer I got the better I could see him. He was definitely majorly good-looking, not like a film star or anything, just sort of normal, really. I was pretty sure he was looking at me too, but then when we were close enough to each other to see the other person clearly, he looked down and walked past me.

My first reaction was disappointment, then I realized that it was no wonder he'd looked down. He was only about my age but he must have thought I was much older, all tarted up like this. I blushed at the thought. Oh well, at least I knew now that I looked sixteen, which was what I'd set out to do. All the same, it was a real downer that on the one occasion I would have preferred to look my normal self, I didn't. I shrugged and began running again. After all it was doubtful that I'd ever see that boy again.

I arrived puffing and panting outside the café to find Tash looking very anxious. "I thought you weren't coming after all," were her first words.

"Sorry. It took me longer than I thought to get this lot on," I said, rolling my eyes to show I wasn't at all pleased with my appearance.

"Well, you'd certainly pass for a sixteen-year-old," was all Tash said.

"Is he here? Have you seen him?" I asked, feeling my heart beating a little faster again.

"It's hard to tell, but I don't think so," Tash replied, peering in through the window.

And that was when he appeared! Not inside the café, but outside, as if from nowhere. He was in his late twenties, I guessed, rather peculiar-looking, tall and thin.

"Evening, ladies," he commented, but he wasn't looking at Tash at all, just at me.

"Hello," we both mumbled, slipping off round the back as he pushed open the door to go into the café.

I grabbed Tash's arm. "Was that him?"

She nodded, her eyes round.

"Right, I'll see you tomorrow, Tash. I'm going to take over from Andy now. But can you do me a favour? At exactly eight-forty-five, phone our place. Let it ring once, then ring off. Rachel's going to do the rest."

"Yes, that's no problem. But Fen, what will Jan think?"

"Dunno."

"You're mad, Fen," was Tash's parting shot, as

I pushed open the back door that goes into the café's kitchen.

"You're the second person to tell me I'm mad in under half an hour," I answered in a hurried whisper.

"That proves it's true, then."

I didn't answer. Just prepared myself to face the music.

Chapter 2

Andy was slicing a quiche in the kitchen as I walked in. Jan was nowhere to be seen.

"I think it's best if you just go quickly, Andy. I can deal with Jan better on my own."

Andy was staring at me open-mouthed. I suddenly realized what she was staring at. My appearance.

"Oh … this…" I said, feeling embarrassed all of a sudden, as I looked down at myself, knowing that the worst part of my appearance was actually my face, all daubed with make-up like that.

"You've got a boyfriend, haven't you, Fen?" asked Andy, as though everything was suddenly clear to her.

"No, I haven't!"

"Then why are you dolled up to the eyeballs like that?"

"I can't explain. There isn't time. But I will tomorrow."

"Come off it, Fen. You've got a boyfriend. It's obvious. Or…" Her eyes were gleaming thoughtfully, and my heart was beating like mad because I just wanted her to get going quickly before Jan came into the kitchen. "Or maybe you've got your eye on someone and he's coming here tonight."

I was beginning to feel really irritated by then. "There's no boyfriend, all right? This is serious, Andy. Just let me take over before Jan comes in and refuses to let me swap."

"But what will you say when she finds I've gone without a word and you're here in my place. Are you going to pretend I've suddenly been taken ill or something?"

"We can't pull that stunt again and get away with it," I commented, thinking back to the awful time when we'd had to prevent Andy's dad from knowing that she was working at the café, when he was actually sitting large as life at one of the tables and Andy was in the kitchen washing up! I shivered at the memory.

"All right, I'm going," Andy suddenly announced, obviously taking my shiver as one of anxiety.

"Don't worry, I know what I'm going to say," I told her quickly.

"Well, it better be good … and your explanation tomorrow better be good too, Fen."

"It will be – and don't worry, *you'll* get the wages, not me."

"Good luck," she said, looking straight into my eyes to show me she wasn't really as rattled as she may have seemed. Then she went out.

"Thanks," I smiled back. Andy was a great judge of situations, and I knew that, in the end, she'd believed that I couldn't be all tarted up for the sake of a boy.

I was just contemplating the quiche, and realizing that I'd no idea what I was supposed to be doing when Jan walked in. Her eyes widened with surprise, then narrowed with mistrust – or was it just annoyance – when she saw me standing there instead of Andy.

"What's going on, Fen? Where's Andy?" she asked, frowning as her eyes travelled down to my feet then slowly back up to my face. I blushed because I wasn't comfortable with my image, then quickly recited the words I'd been practising.

"We've got to do this play in assembly tomorrow morning. It's all about 'Moving on'. It wasn't supposed to be our turn, but at the last minute the PSE teacher changed her mind, so we've only had this evening to sort it all out, you see. Tash and the others are going to tell Andy what we've done so far, and I've already learnt my bit, so that's why I'm here instead of Andy. She was going to say bye, but decided she'd better not disturb you."

I smiled at her, because I could tell by her expression that I'd managed to convince her. Although the real reason I smiled at her was because I was feeling guilty about the lie – another one. I tried to keep telling myself that they were only *white* lies.

"I don't know how you manage to fit everything in, you girls. Well done, Fen. I mean, for not leaving me in the lurch. Er … I won't make a big deal of it this once, Fen, but I think a little less make-up in future, hmm?"

Again I blushed because I didn't want Jan to think that I liked the look of myself like this.

"Right!" She suddenly snapped back into action and clicked her fingers in the direction of the quiche. "I'll have that quiche, thanks. And could you bring in a tray of wine glasses from the dishwasher?"

She was off before I could say a word. And half a minute later I was off too. Straight into the lion's den. I didn't look right or left as I put the tray of glasses down on the counter.

"These are for table six. I'll bring the wine. And this is table three's order. Quick as you can, pet."

This was it. I felt rather wobbly on my legs as I went over to table three. Thinking it was better not to make eye contact with anyone, I just stared

23

at the bit of carpet I was about to walk on. As I put the food down in front of the two men, they both said "Thank you" and I had to look at them then. Jan had drilled us thoroughly on looking at the customers properly, and being pleasant and polite at all times. I smiled at them both, noting with relief that neither of them was Inspector Starebear!

I rushed back and put the glasses for table six on the tray, wondering why on earth I hadn't put them on the tray in the first place. The trouble was I was too nervous to think straight. Jan followed and poured out the wine because, of course, we're not allowed to serve alcohol at our age.

A quick glance at the men at that table showed that once again I was in luck, but then all my safe little feelings dissolved as a voice from a nearby table said, "Could I have a coffee, please, when you've got a moment?" I recognized the voice and turned slowly towards him. I was right. It was the man from outside – the one who had been staring at Tash the last time. I had to look cool and confident and *sixteen* at all costs.

"Certainly," I replied as calmly and maturely as I could, while trying not to snatch his empty wine glass up too hastily.

When I returned with the coffee I realized with horror that my hand was trembling, and it didn't improve when I noticed the amusement in his eyes as he watched me.

"I don't know," he said with a casual smile, "the waitresses these days get younger and younger."

It was like a kick in the gut. He'd only spoken two sentences to me and already I had been proved right. He was here to check up on our age. It was tempting to quickly assure him I was sixteen, but I stopped myself because that would just sound plain suspicious. Instead I gave him a sort of sassy smile. (To use a word that Jaimini's mum always uses.)

"You look about the same age as my niece – fourteen."

There was no putting it off any longer. I had to say it, though I made sure I had my back to Jan in case she happened to be lip-reading at that moment. "Well, I'm sixteen, actually."

"Sixteen, eh?" he said, very slowly, and his eyes were still filled with amusement, which made me feel stupid, as though he was laughing at me. Then, without warning, his expression suddenly went straight into neutral as he said, "Well, don't let me keep you. It's certainly busy in here tonight."

"Yes, business is great," I agreed, trying to sound adult, but I noticed that Jan was very close by, and I couldn't stop wondering for ages why the man had changed his attitude towards me. Was it because he realized I wasn't sixteen, but he thought that Jan didn't know that, so he was trying to help me keep the secret?

As the evening wore on I felt more and more uncomfortable about the man. He hadn't said another word to me, but I was continually aware of his eyes on me. I'm certain I wasn't imagining it. Every time I glanced up, he seemed to be looking at me. And what made it worse was that whenever our eyes met, it was always me who had to look away first.

It was a wonderful relief when he went, about forty minutes later. He had been the only person in the café to have been sitting on his own.

"What was that man saying to you earlier on?" Jan asked me abruptly, at one point.

"He commented on how busy it was," I answered, carefully.

"You have to be more careful about chatting to customers in the evening, Fen," Jan said, sounding unsure of herself. "You ... you don't want to give the wrong impression."

I certainly agreed with her there. I thought I'd been giving the right impression, pretending to be sixteen. Little did I know. I just nodded in reply and said "Mm," because we were on dangerous ground here and I wanted to get off it.

*　*　*

"Where's Danny then?" were Mum's first words when she opened the door. It was ten o'clock and I'd had to ring the bell.

"He's gone," I answered.

I'd actually completely forgotten about Danny. Jan had asked me at the café if Dad was coming to collect me. I knew that she'd never agree to let me walk home alone, and I realized that the only alternative would be to wait for her to take me, which would make me too late. So I said that Dad *was* coming and that I'd seen our car outside. Luckily she didn't check up and I was able to go off without any problems. I can't say that I enjoyed the journey home, though. Most of it was well lit, but all the same, there was something about that man that had completely unnerved me.

"Have you been crying?" Mum asked, peering at my face. I'd gone into the loo and rubbed vigorously at my make-up before leaving the café, so I expect I did look rather blotchy.

"Tash and I were trying on different make-up," I said, briefly.

"I thought you were supposed to be doing geography."

"Yes, we did that first."

"Well, Danny made a fast getaway, didn't he?"

Mum was sounding suspicious and I wasn't surprised.

"There's something on TV he wanted to get back for, so I said I was fine for the last few metres."

"Oh," was all Mum said to that. I called out "Night," to Dad, then went upstairs wearily, and plonked down on my bed staring into space, deep in thought. It was no good, I couldn't keep this up. I did a quick tot up of how many lies, however small, I'd had to tell in just one evening. No, I definitely couldn't carry on like this. I hated telling lies. Worse than that, I hated myself when I told lies.

I lay awake for ages that night, because it's difficult to sleep when you hate yourself.

The next morning break I rounded up all my friends and we went down to our usual outside meeting place on the netball courts, which are well away from where most people go at break times. The only bad thing about our meeting place is that the staffroom looked out over it, but it was several metres away, so no teacher would be able to hear what we were saying. In fact, the teachers rarely looked out of the window.

"Fen's got something to tell you," Tash announced, importantly. Tash and I had already agreed before assembly that I would come clean, then we'd have six brains instead of two working on the problem.

"Look, I'm really sorry," I began, already feeling the relief of unburdening myself and confessing that I'd been deceitful, "but, the thing is, it's against the law for anyone under sixteen to work after seven o'clock in the evening, but I pretended to Jan that Mum rang the LEA, you see, and that she found out that it didn't matter after all, as it wasn't like a proper job, when each of us would only be doing it once every six weeks…"

I glanced round to see how they were taking it. They were all frowning and looking extremely serious – even Luce. I began to speak a little less confidently.

"Then I pretended to Mum that Jan had phoned the LEA … and that they had told her the same thing…"

I stopped, because it seemed impossible to go on with them all staring at me intently like that.

"Well, actually *my* mum and dad were worried about me working in the evening at my age," commented Leah. "I heard them discussing it in the kitchen, but they finished up by saying that it must be all right, because Jan wouldn't have been so silly as not to have investigated something as basic as that before agreeing to it."

"Yeah, my parents asked me the same thing," Jaimini put in, "and I said it must be all right because Jan would have gone into it properly before taking us on."

There was a pause, then Luce spoke.

"That's great, isn't it," she said, sarcastically, tossing her hair back. "I don't even get to have my go, and we've got to knock it on the head."

"Not necessarily," I replied.

"Oh, come on, Fen," Tash chipped in, quickly. "We can't carry on. We could be in deep trouble."

"And Jan would be in even deeper trouble," Jaimini pointed out.

"Jaimini's right," said Leah. "It's not fair on Jan. You'll just have to tell her that you've found out after all that it's not allowed."

"What do you think, Andy?" I asked, as she was the only one who hadn't given her view.

"Dangerous," she said, quietly. "Dangerous."

Andy rarely wasted words, and on this occasion, I didn't know if she'd intended to scare us, but her one stark word certainly had that effect on us all.

"You're on duty today at the café after school, aren't you?" Tash asked, turning to me with an urgent look of appeal in her eyes. I nodded. "Well, why don't you tell Jan straight away? You'll have to, Fen."

The others were nodding gravely. I felt torn. You see, it just wasn't as easy as all that. I mean, how could I waltz in and say, "Oh, by the way Jan, you know I said that Mum found out it was perfectly legal for us all to work late? Well, she was mistaken actually, because it's perfectly *ill*egal after all!" It was ridiculous. Jan would be furious. She'd realize I'd been blatantly lying *and* putting the café at risk in the process.

And then there was the problem of what I would say to Mum. That Jan had changed her mind and decided not to have us working there after all? My head was spinning with thoughts and worries, and the biggest worry of all kept coming up to the surface. Sooner or later Jan and Mum would talk to each other and compare notes. Then they'd both realize how manipulative I'd been. That would probably make Jan sack me altogether so I'd never be able to work in the café again! No, there was *no way* I could go through with it.

"Well?" Andy suddenly cut into my troubled thoughts.

They were waiting for my reassurance. It would be impossible to explain all that had been going on inside my head for the last thirty seconds. "Yeah, OK, I'll tell her," I replied with a sigh. You'd think I'd released them from having to do school exams or something, the way they all let out their breath at the same moment.

I said I was going to the loo then, because I figured it would have been too hard to hang around with them for the rest of break, keeping up the pretence that I was going to speak to Jan after school. Because I wasn't going to, you see. I couldn't.

Exactly what I *was* going to do, I had no idea. I only knew I didn't dare tell Jan the truth. I'd just have to take it a week at a time, and maybe I'd manage to get Tash to see my point of view, then there'd be two of us keeping a secret from the other four. I might have to invent a Wednesday evening youth club for Mum's benefit. It would be like walking along a tightrope, but even that would be preferable to losing Jan's and Mum's trust *and* my job.

After school, the others insisted on coming down to the café with me. Those of us who aren't working often go down to the café and have a Coke or whatever, but I had the feeling on this particular day that my friends were there to check up on me. They wanted to be sure that I owned up to Jan.

Jan wasn't in the kitchen when I went in through the back door, but Kevin the chef was. Kevin is about twenty-one, small, dark and wiry. He works out at the gym a lot so he's very fit and strong. Jan says he's a brilliant chef, and now we girls have got to know him, we think so too.

Kevin is also a very kind person, but the complete opposite of a busybody. He lives in his own little world and always seems happy with life.

We've all had a giggle at one time or another over Kevin's sudden outbursts of strange, tuneless singing, but he pays us back by taking the mickey out of us mercilessly and cracking witty jokes at our expense.

The interesting thing about Kevin, though, is that although he appears quite superficial, underneath he has another whole layer which is really sincere, understanding and protective.

"Watcha Nell!" was Kevin's opening line as usual. (My full name is Fenella Brooks, so that's where Kevin got the "Nell" bit from.) I'd long since given up protesting when Kevin used this nickname for me. It only made him use it all the more if he thought I objected.

"Watcha, Kev. Doing a bit of cooking for a change?" I gave him a sarcastic smile which he totally ignored as he neatly rolled up an omelette and tipped it on to a large plate with some chips.

"Table seven's ready, Jan," he told her as she came in through the swing door.

"Hi, pet. You're not sick of the place yet I hope!" she grinned. "Two sessions on the trot and all that."

I just smiled and probably went a bit pink because this was the moment when the others thought I'd be telling her we couldn't carry on doing the Wednesday evenings. In fact, Jan had given me the perfect lead in. I could have simply

33

said, "Well actually, Mum thinks it's a bit much with homework and everything, you know. And some of the other parents are feeling the same…"

Go on, Fen. Just say it! I urged myself silently. But it was too late. She'd gone.

"Jump to it, Nell. The washing-up beckons," quipped Kevin, so I put an apron on, ran the taps hard into the sink, while squirting tons of washing-up liquid to make a huge white mountain of foam. Then I dabbed my finger into it and tried to work out ways of approaching Jan.

It had occurred to me that the others wouldn't stop pestering me until they knew I had spoken to Jan, so I had had to take a rain check on my thoughts of the previous day that I wouldn't own up. It was all so complicated, especially when I considered pretending to tell her just to stop the others from going on at me all the time.

What a stupid situation to be in, I thought, aggressively plunging a greasy frying pan into the hot, soapy water.

"Temper temper!" said Kevin, who must have had eyes in the back of his head, because he was frying beefburgers and I swear he hadn't turned round from the Aga.

Perhaps I ought to ask Kevin's advice, I thought briefly, then changed my mind almost immediately because it was too complicated to explain, and knowing Kevin he wouldn't grasp

34

the importance of keeping my secret and he'd go blurting out to Jan something like, "Fen's been telling porky pies, Jan. She knows perfectly well that under-sixteens aren't allowed to work in the evenings, so you'd better sack this load of thirteen-year-olds and get someone else quick!"

About five minutes later when I'd attacked at least eight fatty pans, Jan came up to me sounding very excited and said, "Whoever's on next Wednesday evening is going to have fun!"

I gulped. Here was another chance to confess. "Why is that?" I asked weakly.

"Magic evening!" she said, eyes gleaming.

"Magic!" I repeated, forgetting my own problems for a moment. "That sounds great!"

"It will be great. I've got someone who's a member of the magic circle coming. His name is Raj."

"Raj? He's Indian, then?"

"That's right, and quite a big name. It should be fantastic. I've just been telling the others."

"Oh…" I stammered. "Wh – what did they say?"

"They said they couldn't remember whose turn it was. To be perfectly honest I think their minds were on something else. They were acting very strangely." Jan chuckled. "There's a very nice-looking lad in there, and Luce in particular can't take her eyes off him!"

"Lucy Locket lost her pocket," Kevin burst out in the most appalling tuneless snatch of song you've ever heard. Jan and I laughed, then out she rushed like a whirlwind, scooping up another order on her way. Jan was certainly in an excellent mood.

A magic evening. It sounded brilliant. Suddenly I knew exactly what I would do. I would tell Jan that the reason the others were acting very vaguely about who was on duty was because next Wednesday was a bit of a problem for all of them, so we'd agreed that I'd do it again, and I didn't mind at all. In fact I was delighted.

Then I'd tell the others I couldn't possibly let Jan down for the magic evening, so I would do *just* that one. And I'd promise to tell her the very next day that we couldn't carry on any longer. Whether or not I'd have the guts to do it when the time came, I didn't know, but I'd cross that bridge when I came to it. For now, my problem was solved.

When Jan came in a minute later, I delivered the exact speech I'd planned and she didn't seem at all perturbed that I'd be working on Wednesday evening yet again. I allowed myself to relax – just a tiny bit.

"Be a pet and take table three's order, Fen," Jan said a moment later.

I swung into the café with a full tray for table

three and nearly went flying because there was a foot sticking out that definitely hadn't been there a moment earlier.

"What the…?" I began.

"Whoops! Nearly tripped!" came a boy's voice imitating a high-pitched, silly girl's voice. This was followed by great guffaws of laughter from three other boys.

"What a pathetic thing to do," I snapped, turning on the ringleader, who was a thin boy with a big grin and sticky-out ears.

"'What a pathetic thing to do,'" he mimicked me, in the same high-pitched voice, which made my blood boil. Apart from being angry I also felt frustrated because I was standing there with a full tray, which left me at a distinct disadvantage, so I quickly delivered the order to table three, then went over to Tash and the others when I heard my name being whispered loudly by Luce. They drew me conspiratorially into their little circle.

"Have you seen that gorgeous specimen in the corner?" Luce asked me, narrowing her eyes as though she was in ecstasy.

I was about to turn round but Luce hissed, "Don't look now. It'll be obvious we've been talking about him if you do. I think he goes to Woodman's. He's definitely not from Cableden." (Woodman's is another big school about five miles out of Cableden.)

"And by the way," Tash added in a whisper. "Have you seen that distinctly *un*gorgeous specimen in the other corner?"

"What?" I asked, feeling confused by all this talk of specimens.

"You'll see," Tash replied, with pursed lips.

"Don't look at him. Look at my gorgeous one," Luce hissed, grabbing my arm and squeezing it in rapture.

"Let go, Luce, I've got stuff to do."

Jaimini prised Luce's fingers off my arm as Luce was gazing into the middle distance with a euphoric look in her eyes. I started to go back to the kitchen, trying to get a good look round as subtly as possible on the way.

How I got to the kitchen without dropping my tray or crumpling to the ground I don't know, because in one corner of the café sat the boy I'd passed on the way to the café the previous evening. And in the other corner sat Inspector Starebear, his eyes full of that look of cool amusement, following me as I walked, and making me blush furiously. Then in between those two was the table with Big Ears and his pathetic pals.

"Oooh, look at Matthew," piped up Big Ears to his mates. "Can't get his eyes off the waitress. But she'd rather play footsie with me, Matthew, that's the problem," he called a little more loudly, which attracted a few customers' attention.

"I wasn't playing footsie," I protested, furiously.

"'I wasn't playing footsie,'" came the dreaded imitation, and this time, unfortunately, it sounded just like me because as I'd been so cross, my voice had come out in a silly high-pitched sort of whine. This of course made the other three boys at the table fall about hysterically.

"Oooh dear, Matthew doesn't look very pleased, does he?" one of the others said, in a mocking tone.

"That's because he's been struck by an arrow from Cupid's bow," Big Ears said, obviously thinking he was being really witty.

"Oh, shut up!" I said, trying to sound dismissive, because I couldn't think of anything else to say.

"Oooh listen, Hot Lips here is defending Macho Man Matthew. Whatever next?" the grinning ringleader went on. There didn't seem to be any stopping him. I glanced at the boy called Matthew and saw that he looked really uncomfortable. I instantly wanted to spring to his defence, but that stupid Big Ears would make me pay for it if I did, so I decided to disappear before things could get any worse.

"I'll get you back, just you wait, Big Ears," I hissed at him, then I shot through the swing door to the kitchen.

Chapter 3

Once inside the kitchen I took deep breaths and tried to regain my self-control. I busied myself unloading the dishwasher and wiping and hanging up all the pans I'd washed. Seeing that boy again – Matthew – had given me a real jolt. He'd obviously noticed me, and that made me really happy. I wondered if he realized that I was the girl he had seen the previous evening. And if so, whatever had he made of my dramatic and sudden image change? The truth is I've never fancied a real live boy before. Of course there are quite a lot of good-looking pop stars, but this was the first time I'd seen anyone my own age who'd had such an effect on me.

On the other hand, that horrible man at the other corner table was obviously still checking up on me. He probably thought he'd catch me out by seeing me in daylight with no make-up on. And that was precisely what he'd done, too. Then there was Big Ears and his mates. They made me sick, but at least they didn't scare me like that man did.

If only I could quickly borrow some make-up from someone. Normally Becky would be working at the café with Jan and me, and I would have been able to borrow some make-up from her. It's always either Becky or Mark working at the same time as us, but apparently Becky had phoned in ill at the last minute and Jan had said we'd manage all right without her just this once.

It was busy, but Jan was on such a high that she seemed to be moving even faster than usual and was practically doing the work of two people. There wasn't anyone else I could borrow make-up from because Jan didn't carry any around with her. But… Yes, of course, Luce would have some in her school bag.

What a ridiculous situation to be in! Half of me wanted to get make-up on quickly for the benefit of that awful man, but the other half wanted to stay normal and natural for the benefit of a boy who might not even give me a second glance – who might not even still be sitting there… Oh, no!

I took a deep breath and plunged back into the café, deliberately averting my face from starey-features, but trying at the same time to look suitably cool for gorgeous-features. I stole the teeniest glance in his direction and very nearly rose up to the ceiling because, guess what? He was looking at me! He obviously didn't want me to know that though, because he immediately looked down at his empty plate. The Big Ears brigade were hunched and giggling over a magazine or something, so they didn't notice me come in, thank goodness.

At Luce's table, I tried not to show I was impressed by the boy, even when Leah said, "He can't take his eyes off you, Fen."

"Who?" I asked, trying for a look of mild bewilderment that I thought would be suitable.

"The boy in the corner, of course," answered Leah.

"And neither," said Tash, looking serious and speaking pointedly, "can that bloke in the other corner."

"I know," I replied. "That's why I came over here. Have you got any make-up I can borrow, Luce?"

"What for?" asked Luce, looking puzzled.

"To try to look older, of course."

"Don't you think it's a bit too late for that now?" Andy pointed out.

"Andy's right," agreed Jaimini. "You'd only be drawing attention to yourself if you suddenly piled on the make-up."

42

"And what would Jan think?" Leah added.

"Yeah, you're right," I conceded, feeling secretly relieved that the decision had been made for me and I didn't have to start ruining my chances with Matthew.

"Talking of Jan, have you told her yet?" asked Tash, who wouldn't get off my case.

"No, but I'm going to."

They all looked a bit tight-lipped so I quickly launched into my explanation.

"The thing is, I couldn't let her down next Wednesday, when she's so excited about her magic evening, so I told her that I would work that Wednesday, too. I said that by total coincidence you lot had all got other things on."

"But that's not fair," Luce began, indignantly.

"I've already explained. We can't afford for that inspector guy in the corner to suspect there are under-age girls working here. He thinks I'm sixteen, so let's not push our luck by trying to pass the rest of you off as sixteen-year-olds as well," I said, rather stroppily.

"Sure he's going to think you're sixteen when you're over here talking with us lot," said Andy, sarcastically.

"I've got an idea," said Jaimini, excitedly. "Pretend Leah is your sister. She looks the most like you. That means you're over here talking to your sister and her friends."

"Good idea," I agreed, enthusiastically. "Come on, Luce, you're the actress. Get acting. Say something."

"Right," Luce said, immediately psyching herself into the mood, as she always did when anything dramatic was involved. "Leah," she instructed, "wait till Fen's almost reached the kitchen, then call out, 'What time shall I tell Mum you'll be home, Fen?' Then Fen, you call back, 'I won't be late, I've got tons of work for my mocks.' Got that?"

"You're brilliant, Luce," Jaimini congratulated her best friend, warmly. "That'll be much more convincing than a load of make-up. Come on, then. Let's see it in action, and don't, for goodness' sake, say it if Jan's listening!"

As soon as Jan had disappeared into the kitchen, off I went, feeling more torn in two than I'd ever felt before. If I kept up the lie that I was sixteen I'd be saving my skin as far as Jan and the café were concerned, but I could also say goodbye to the only boy I'd ever fancied, before I'd even said hello. What a position to be in. I stole a little glance at Matthew then, and my heart missed a beat because he called out, "'Scuse me…"

I realized he wanted me to go over to him, and as that realization came to me, all thoughts of pretending that Leah was my sister left me. I've never concentrated so hard on trying to walk perfectly – not too quickly and eagerly, but not too slowly either. Not too upright, but with good posture all the same.

"Could I have one of those cakes, please?" he asked.

"Yeah, sure," I answered, instantly regretting the "sure" and wishing I could change it to "course". "Any particular one? You can come and choose, if you want."

"Yeah, OK."

Feeling five pairs of eyes from our table, one pair from the corner table, and by now four other pairs from Big Ears' table, all boring into me, I walked with Matthew over to the cakes. He was about three centimetres taller than me and it felt so nice having him at my side.

"Do you work here every day?" he asked me, sounding a bit unsure of himself, which had the immediate effect of making me feel much more self-confident.

"Once or twice a week," I answered, with a friendly smile.

"Are you working tomorrow?" he asked.

"Not tomorrow, no."

"Go on, go for it, Matthew," the dreaded voice came floating over.

"Yeah, go for it, Matthew. You'll be all right there, mate!"

God, they made me sick.

By this time Matthew and I were standing in front of the cakes, and I felt as though I was poised on the end of a diving board waiting for a whistle to tell me to dive, because I was aware of this being the build-up to being asked out.

I just knew he was about to do it, and I was willing him to get on with it quickly before he changed his mind, or before one of those stupid boys said something to embarrass him too much. It was incredible that he preferred me to any of the others. Most boys fancied Leah or Jaimini. This would be such a brilliant win for me. So why wasn't he asking me? Why was he surveying the cakes so earnestly? I decided to help him. I leaned sideways against the counter and ran my hand through my hair, at the same time giving him the most dazzling smile I could, while softly asking what school he went to.

"Woodman's," he answered, returning my smile, which sent me to heaven and back because we were looking straight into each others' eyes and we both knew we fancied one another.

"I'm Fen, by the way," I said, trying to imitate the very sexiest girls on *Baywatch*.

"I was wondering whether you were free…"

Matthew never got any further than that because I was suddenly aware of a movement behind him. It was the man at the corner table. He'd moved his chair very slightly so that

Matthew's back wasn't blocking his view and he could see me. Our eyes met and I felt sick. The look he gave me was challenging and mean. In that one second all my rapt feelings about Matthew slid away and dissolved. Those horrible eyes were saying, "I see, so you're sixteen, are you? A sixteen-year-old girl who fancies a thirteen-year-old boy. Don't make me laugh."

I must have looked as though I'd seen a ghost because Matthew whipped his head round to see what I was looking at, then immediately turned back to me. I had to make a decision. And extremely quickly. Either I kept up the pretence of being sixteen and losing Matthew, or I admitted to being thirteen, which would mean losing my job, probably. Or, at the very least, it would mean big trouble for me.

It was at that second that Leah's voice came floating over.

"What time shall I tell Mum you'll be home, Sis?"

She'd added the "Sis". I was sure that hadn't been in the original script. This was my cue to answer, but my throat felt so tight, I didn't think I'd manage more than a croak.

Matthew was pointing to a cake.

"Er ... I'll have that one, please," he said, and I noticed two high spots of red on his cheeks.

Stupidly I let my eyes slip back to the corner

table. The man's expression had eased back into that cool, amused look. But the intensity of his gaze made my heart beat with fear that he was just biding his time, and then he was somehow going to make me suffer.

I still hadn't answered Leah, because I didn't know what to do, but the decision was taken out of my hands with Leah's next words.

"I'll tell her you'll be late because you've got your mocks to revise for, haven't you?"

Matthew turned round again and looked behind him. He must have noticed my wandering gaze. When he turned back to me his whole face had changed. Poor Matthew. He'd seen that hateful, horrible man leering at me, he'd seen me looking at the man, he'd heard what Leah had said, he'd put two and two together and made five.

I wanted to scream out at the top of my voice, "NO! NO! Matthew, you've got it all wrong. I'm not sixteen. I don't fancy that revolting thing in the corner. It's *you* I'm interested in." But of course I couldn't. I just reached into the tall, glass cake display cupboard and began to slide Matthew's choice on to the cake slice.

"It's all right," he mumbled. "I've changed my mind." He made a big thing of looking at his watch, but I knew it was to hide his embarrassment. Then suddenly the café was filled with uproarious laughter. I swung round to see Big Ears and his friends collapsing over each other as though they were watching the comedy of the year. Then they started clapping and jeering.

"Nice try, Matthew. Stick to girls your own age next time," the voice that I hated most burst forth.

"Shut up, Barry," Matthew replied, as two of the other boys slapped each others' hands in a triumphant gesture.

Jan emerged from the kitchen at that point. She took in the situation in a microsecond, and looking absolutely furious, strode up to the boy called Barry, yanked him to his feet, marched him to the front door – the others following meekly in his wake – opened the door wide and ordered them all out. The three followers scuttled off like frightened little kids, but Barry stayed there grinning through the glass at Matthew. I swore to myself at that moment that I would make him suffer one day. One day I really would.

The other customers slowly returned to their own conversations, the brief drama over. Poor Matthew pulled two coins out of his pocket, and thrust them at me.

"That enough?" he barked, without looking at me.

"I'll get your change," I said a little shakily.

"Don't bother," he answered, so softly I hardly

heard him. Then he left the café and joined the still-grinning Barry. What a weird friendship that was. How could a good-looking person like Matthew, who also seemed sensible and intelligent, hang about with such a prat as that Barry? It was very strange. It was also over. I sighed a big sigh and threw a quick glance at Leah and saw that she was biting her lip and her shoulders were hunched up. Good. I hoped she felt very guilty. I knew it wasn't her fault, but I couldn't help feeling furious with everybody. I was stuck in a hopeless situation.

My dragging feet somehow took me into the kitchen, where an awful cloud of depression hung over me until the end of my duty. For fifteen miserable minutes I worked silently in the kitchen. Occasionally, Jan crashed in and out, apparently unaffected by the incident with those boys because she was still humming away.

Kevin, with his sixth sense, seemed to know there was something wrong with me and that I didn't want to discuss it, because he left me alone and didn't even give me the benefit of his scintillating wit or his amazing singing voice.

When I had to go into the café later, the others had all gone. I knew that anyway, because Jan had told me earlier that they all said "Bye" and "See you tomorrow". The man had gone too. And when six o'clock came, so did I.

On arriving home, it was obvious Mum was in a bad mood, but I couldn't work out why at first. Emmy kept going up to her and offering kisses, saying, "Try to smile a bit, Mummy. Why are you such an old grumpy lump?" Of course, that simply made matters worse.

"Be quiet, Emmy," Rachel said. "Mummy's cross with Fen. It's nothing to do with you." I couldn't bear the way Rachel said that. She sounded so smug and pleased with herself.

"What have I done now?" I asked Mum, with just the teeniest feeling of alarm creeping up on me.

"It's more what you haven't done," she replied as she tipped steaming pasta into a big dish.

"Shall I set the table, Mummy?" asked Rachel, who was really getting on my nerves with her goody-goody act.

"You'd better not," I couldn't resist commenting vehemently. "You might bang your halo on something, and we don't want it falling off, do we?"

"There's no need to talk like that, Fen," snapped Mum, turning to face me. "I'm not too happy to find you've been lying to me, that's all."

I felt my cheeks getting hot as my heart beat a little faster.

"You may well look embarrassed, young lady," went on Mum. "What I want to know is, where

51

were you last night, if you weren't at Tash's house?"

My mouth formed an "O" of surprise because this wasn't at all what I'd thought she was going to say. I was completely taken off my guard.

"Well?" said Mum. Then quite suddenly she softened. "Look love, if you've got a boyfriend, I don't mind. And neither does Dad. But what we're both really worried about is if you're going behind our backs. You can bring him here, you know. You don't have to go out having secret trysts, and pretending to be at Tash's…"

I was about to protest but Mum was in full flow and I couldn't get a word in edgeways.

"To tell you the truth, I'm not so much cross as disappointed. I thought we didn't have secrets in this house. Dad and I honestly thought you'd tell us if you'd got a boyfriend."

Poor Mum. She looked so sad. I noticed Rachel had only laid about two things on the table, she was going in such slow motion in order to listen to Mum. Emmy, on the other hand, was piling all sorts of things on – mats, serviettes, a fistful of teaspoons, tomato ketchup, vinegar, salad cream, strawberry jam. Mum followed my gaze. And thank goodness she did, because it gave me a bit more time to think about what to say.

"Emmy! What are you doing? We don't need all that lot on the table. Just leave one big mat in the middle and put everything else away." Then she turned to Rachel. "Get some forks out, Rachel."

During that brief time I had made a decision. It was safer to let Mum believe I'd gone out to meet a boy, than to say I'd been to work at the café without asking permission.

"Sorry, Mum," I said, looking down. "It was a load of us – not just me. It wasn't anything… I mean, it wasn't anyone in particular. I won't do it again."

She put her arm round me and gave me a hug, which made me feel really guilty.

"Oh, and Jan's just phoned."

"Jan!" I squeaked, because I didn't think I could take many more shocks.

"Yes. Apparently that magician, Raj, can't make next Wednesday after all, but has offered Saturday at seven o'clock."

"Saturday at seven! But the café's not even open then!"

"Not usually, no. But just this once Jan's decided to make an exception. She reckons an awful lot of people are going to be disappointed if she cancels him."

I felt a slight rush of panic as I remembered the cross-country, but I calmed down when I remembered it was due to start at one o'clock. It wouldn't be a problem doing both. All the same, it was bringing forward the dreaded moment of talking to Jan.

"But why can't she just postpone it to another Wednesday evening?" I asked Mum.

"It seems that Jan and Raj must have been talking at cross purposes, because Raj thought Jan meant Wednesday afternoon. He's got a regular gig, as they call it, on Wednesday evenings. It was a jolly good job he happened to phone Jan back to confirm the address of the café, otherwise he would have turned up next Wednesday afternoon."

Mum was gabbling on chirpily and never quite coming to the point of this story.

"So why did Jan phone?" I eventually managed to ask.

"Oh, because she's rung round all the others very quickly and they're all busy on Saturday, surprisingly enough!"

I felt that now familiar feeling of anxiety looming up on me. Of course the others had said they were busy. They didn't dare to work evenings now they knew the rule about working later than seven o'clock. They were all petrified of that horrible leering inspector. And so was I. But I was in too deep now.

"I'll do it, Mum," I said. "I'd love to."

"I thought you would," Mum said cheerfully. Then her eyes twinkled as she clutched my shoulders. "I was thinking that Dad and I could come along too, Fen. It sounds great fun."

"Oh … right…" I stammered, while thinking *Oh no, Mum! Please don't!*

On the following morning, Friday, I talked to Tash.

"I presume Jan phoned you about doing Saturday evening," she began with a reproving look, rather like one of Mum's, actually.

"Yes, she did," I answered, coolly. "I said I'd do it."

"So when are you going to tell Jan the truth, Fen?" Tash asked me insistently.

"I'll tell her straight after the magic evening, I promise," I replied, rashly. I'd actually decided to leave it till the following day. Jan wouldn't be so fraught on a Sunday.

"Good," said Tash, "then we'll all be able to relax again."

"There's nothing to worry about. That bloke believes I'm sixteen, and he's never going to catch any of you lot at work in the evening."

"But you can't do Wednesday evenings for ever. Your mum won't let you."

"Look, Tash, I've promised I'll tell Jan after the magic evening, OK?"

"Yes. Sorry, I won't mention it again. Let's change the subject. Have you seen those lovely trousers they've got in Kool Kit?"

"No."

"I'm going to buy a pair on Saturday afternoon. I've finally saved enough money. Why don't you come with me, Fen?"

"I can't on Saturday. I've got that cross-country event at Lowerden Forest School."

"Where exactly is Lowerden Forest?"

"About half-an-hour on the minibus, I think."

"Who else is going from our school?"

"Only Andy from our year."

"Are there lots of schools entering?"

"Ten, I think, including one or two really good ones."

"I bet they won't have any runners as good as you and Andy," Tash said, warmly. She was always very proud of me whenever I did any running events. Cross-country was the only sort of running that I was any good at. Andy, on the other hand, could sprint or run long distance equally well. The PE teachers at our school were all very impressed by her. I knew they were also hoping that I'd do well for the school team too, but I nearly always came in second after Andy in our school cross-country runs.

"Don't be disappointed if you do less well than usual, Fen," Mr Cobb had said to me. "You'll find there's some excellent competition at this level."

I'd assured him I wasn't even expecting to

come in the first ten, and that I was just pleased to have been chosen for the team. He hadn't said anything like that to Andy, so maybe he secretly hoped she'd win. You had to be fourteen or under to enter the event, but nobody would be under twelve, because there was a separate race for that age group.

"I'm going out after school today to train," I told Tash.

"I thought you weren't supposed to train the day before the event," Tash said.

"You're right. I'm not doing flat out training, just a bit of jogging, that's all."

Through my mind flashed a picture of me and Matthew standing in front of the cake display in the café. I could still hear his voice. "Are you working tomorrow?" Maybe I'd go to the café after all and skip training... No, there'd be no point. I'd killed stone dead any hope of getting Matthew interested in me.

"Whose turn is it to work today?" I asked Tash.

"Jaimini's."

Tash had decided to go to the café after school with the others, except for Andy, who came down to the rec with me. We did a few warm-up exercises, then started some very slow jogging because we didn't want to damage our muscles and joints for the next day. Andy's jogging speed is slightly faster than mine so we decided to go right round the rec, running in opposite directions. Then we could either stop when we met each other, or if we felt like doing more, we could carry on and stop when we met up for the second time. The rec was pretty huge and we guessed we'd probably have had enough at our first meeting!

So off we went. It was a grey day, not raining or windy but very still and a bit misty. As I jogged along, every tiny sound seemed magnified – my breathing, my footsteps... After a bit I realized that these were the *only* two sounds. I felt like I was miles from nowhere. There weren't even any birds singing or dogs barking.

I glanced around apprehensively, and shivered. I could see a tiny figure on the other side of the rec, but it was too misty for me to be able to make out whether it was Andy or not. I was beginning to wish we'd stayed together now. I didn't like this silent, gloomy stretch of open, endless ground.

As I peered into the grey mist ahead I began to make out a figure. There was a little clump of trees in the distance where children came to play on warm, friendly days, and amongst those trees was the silhouette of a man.

Instinctively I wanted to get away, but if I turned back and started jogging in the other direction, Andy would wonder where on earth I'd got to. I had to keep going, which meant that I *had* to run past him.

Don't show that you're scared, Fen, I told myself firmly. *Just run normally, and if he looks at you, call out "Hi" in a perfectly friendly way. After all, he's probably just out with his dog…* What dog? There wasn't a dog in sight. So what was a man doing among a load of dark trees on a misty day on a deserted rec?

He won't be able to run as hard as you, Fen, I told myself rather unconvincingly. *Well, it won't be long until you're within shouting distance of Andy anyway…* Andy. Where was Andy? She could be anywhere. It was impossible to see further than a few metres.

I was approaching the man. He was standing perfectly still. Perhaps I just imagined it was a man. Perhaps it was really a tree in the shape of a man. I gathered a bit more speed and a lot more courage, and called out "Hi" as cheerfully as I could.

"Well, hello. We meet again," he answered, and I realized with a sickening feeling that it was indeed a man – that awful man from the café.

Chapter 4

"Aren't you going to stop? You look as though you could do with a break."

I gazed determinedly ahead. "Sorry, I can't. I'm training, you see."

"Training?"

I was still jogging, and was almost level with him. "I've got a cross-country competition tomorrow."

His voice took on a new tone. I didn't like it. "All the same, I'm *sure* you're allowed a break, aren't you, Fen?"

He had used my name. How did he know my name? I stopped dead.

"How did you ... know my name?" I asked in a distinctly un-sixteen-year-old way, which I instantly regretted.

"I made a point of finding out," he replied smoothly, with that horrible leer. "Come on, Fen.

Come and sit down. I think you and I need to have a little chat, don't you?"

He leaned against one of the trees and indicated the great thick, fallen branch, which children, including us at one time or another, ran along.

Oh, no! This was it! He was about to tell me he'd found me out. He knew I was under sixteen and had been working late, and he was going to fine me. No, worse than that, he was going to make Mum and Dad pay a huge fine and he was going to stop Jan from opening in the evenings. Maybe he even had the power to shut the place down entirely.

I shivered again, and my legs suddenly felt like jelly. I tried to take a step towards him but I couldn't. I was too scared. The look in his eyes was unnerving me. But if I was scared then, in the next moment I was petrified, because he was slowly approaching me, never taking his eyes off me for one second.

Without hesitation I yelled out at the top of my voice.

"Andy!"

"Who's Andy?" he snapped.

"My friend. We're training together."

"What? Boyfriend?"

"No." And then I thought again. A boyfriend who might appear at any second would surely put him off. "Yes."

But I was too late. He just laughed. "Nice try, Fen."

Now I felt really sick. How utterly stupid I'd been. This was no inspector. This was the kind of man we'd all been warned about time and time again – the type that no one should find themselves alone with in the middle of nowhere.

Everything was beginning to fall into place now. After all the warnings we'd received at school *and* at primary school, after all the times we'd been told and told *never* to speak to strangers, here I was in the worst situation possible. And the very worst thing of all was that it had been *my* fault. The man had obviously thought I'd been leading him on by saying I was older than I was. Oh, what a mess. What a complete and utter mess!

Oh, please let Andy get here quickly, I prayed silently. *If you'll just let Andy get here in the next ten seconds, I promise I'll tell Jan the truth and I'll never, ever, work in the evening again, not even the magic evening.*

My heart was banging against my ribs. Where was Andy? I screamed out to her at the top of my voice as I turned and ran and ran from the man as fast as my jelly legs would carry me.

"Fenella? Is that you?" It was another man's voice. Someone I knew. But my mind was crazy and I couldn't work out who it was for a second.

"Yes," I answered in a breathless, quavery voice. Then in the next instant I ran straight into his arms.

"Hey, calm down. It's all right. You're safe now."

It was Mr Blundell, the tech teacher who had seen me on my way to the café on Wednesday evening. He was patting my back rather awkwardly as if he didn't know what to do with me. I knew I was going to be as embarrassed as anything the next day, but it was as though I'd suddenly become a seven-year-old again. I felt safe right where I was so I didn't want to move. In fact, what I wanted to do was to burst into tears.

"You must tell me what's happened, Fen," Mr Blundell was saying. "Has someone tried to hurt you?"

My voice was as bad as my legs. It didn't want to work.

"A man in those trees," I managed in a hoarse whisper as the tears began to come.

"Right," said Mr Blundell. "Stay right here. You're quite safe here. I'll only be gone a minute…"

He strode off towards the trees which were about thirty metres away, but he was back in no time at all.

"He's gone. What happened, Fenella?"

"Omigod!" I suddenly screeched.

"What?"

"Andy! Andy Sorrell. She's out there somewhere. We were running in opposite directions. I should have met her by now."

"Omigod!" he agreed. Then, "Which way?" he demanded.

We set off together. My legs were back to normal now it wasn't my own safety at risk. In fact, they were stronger than ever, and poor Mr Blundell had a job keeping up with me.

"Andy," we both kept yelling out. By now my heart was beating with more than the effects of running hard, but with the terrible fear that something may have happened to Andy.

"Look! Over there!" I cried out. "That's him!"

I couldn't be sure that I was right because all I could make out was the silhouette of a man. Not necessarily the one we were looking for.

"There's no way we're going to be able to catch him up," Mr Blundell puffed. "He's moving fast and he's got too much of a head start. I reckon we scared him off, though."

"But where's Andy?" I wailed.

And then I saw her. She was lying face down, quite still. Mr Blundell and I both dropped to our knees beside her. We whispered her name and asked her if she could hear us. Then I waited with an icy fear creeping over me, as Mr Blundell put his head right down beside her face, which was turned sideways.

"She's breathing," he told me quietly, and I let out a huge sigh of relief, then immediately tensed up again because we didn't know how badly injured she was.

"Fenella, I think it's safest for me to stay here with Agnès. We mustn't move her, you see... What's this? Blood?"

He was right. There was a wound on her forehead, which was actually under her hairline, but the blood had oozed down. There was even a bit on the grass. Mr Blundell took some scrunched up tissues out of his pocket and pressed them against Andy's forehead. He did this very gently so as not to move her at all.

"If you run straight over there, Fenella, you'll get to those houses in no time at all."

"That's Mrs Pemberley's house," I said, my teeth beginning to chatter.

"Go on, then. Quick as you can. Phone for an ambulance, then ask Mrs Pemberley if you can change that sweaty shirt for a big thick jumper. We don't want you catching pneumonia or something."

I did as I was told and ran like the wind, so that when Mrs Pemberley opened her front door she found a panting, sweaty girl on her doorstep.

"Fen! Whatever's the matter? You look as though you've seen a ghost."

I didn't waste time explaining. "Can I phone for an ambulance, please? My friend's on the rec. She's..."

I was in danger of breaking down and I think Mrs Pemberley realized, because she interrupted me and guided me firmly to the phone, saying, "Take slow, deep breaths, Fen. That's right."

I dialled 999, asked for the ambulance service, then gave all the details the woman asked for as calmly and clearly as I could. When I'd finished, Mrs Pemberley presented me with a mug of cocoa and a selection of jumpers. I quickly changed and gulped at the hot chocolate while telling my garbled tale. As soon as I'd finished I announced that I was going back, and Mrs Pemberley insisted on coming too.

Unfortunately that meant I had to go much more slowly than I wanted to, but once we'd reached the rec I ran on ahead.

Mr Blundell had taken off his jacket and laid it down over Andy. He looked frozen. The ambulance arrived only a minute or two later. The ambulance man and woman checked Andy over carefully, while asking Mr Blundell and me all sorts of questions. Next they very gently rolled Andy on to a stretcher as a police car appeared.

"How did the police know?" I whispered to Mr Blundell.

"They always come to the scene of an accident

when there's been an emergency call to the ambulance service or the fire brigade."

The two policemen took a brief statement from me, as well as a description of the man, and they also made a note of my name and address and Andy's too. Then they investigated the turf all round the area where we were gathered.

"Hey, Ed, look at this," called one of the policemen.

We all looked. Suddenly it became very clear what had happened to Andy. There was a large stone sticking up from the ground, and just nearby a little mound of turf had been half-pulled out of the ground.

"Looks to me as though she's tripped on this bumpy bit and gone down on to that stone."

The two policemen had a word with the ambulance people who also had a look at the stone and the dislodged turf, and everyone agreed that that was almost certainly what had happened.

Mr Blundell offered to walk me home, but I insisted on going in the ambulance, so he came with me. The police gave Mrs Pemberley a lift back and she was going to phone my parents. Mum would then phone Andy's mum. Andy's dad was in France, so Andy's poor mum would be all on her own receiving such bad news.

"Is Andy going to be all right?" I asked the ambulance woman on the way to the hospital.

"Yes, she'll be fine. Don't worry." She smiled and reached over to pat my hand.

Andy kept opening her eyes and closing them again. Every time she did I said the same thing. "You're going to be fine, Andy. Don't worry." It somehow comforted me to keep repeating these words that the ambulance lady, whose name was Sue, had said.

Mr Blundell wanted to know more about the man, but he didn't press me to talk if I didn't want to. He explained that he had been using the rec as a short cut to see a friend. Apparently they were writing a textbook together on teaching technology in schools. Normally I would have been really impressed by all of this, but because of the circumstances I could only manage to say "Oh" when he told me.

"That man, Fenella..." he said, lowering his voice so that our conversation would be private.

"I've seen him before in the café where I work..."

"Is that where you were going the other evening when I passed you?"

"Y-yes."

"You work in the evenings?"

"No... I mean, hardly ever. Just once every six weeks ... but I'm not going to any more."

"Wise decision."

I got the impression Mr Blundell was going to say more about that, but then decided not to. It didn't surprise me. I deserved a real lecture, I'd been acting so naïvely and foolishly. But I'd grown up a great deal in only a few hours and right then I only had one thing on my mind – Andy.

I guess we were about two minutes away from the hospital when Andy woke up properly. She seemed to focus on me straight away. Her first words were, "Is this an ambulance, Fen? What's happened to me?"

"Yes, it is, but you're all right," I reassured her. "You must have tripped up on the rec because you've had a nasty bang on the forehead."

Her hand immediately shot up and she touched it tentatively. "I can feel it. It's like an egg." She looked at her fingers with distaste. "Ugh! Blood! So where am I going in an ambulance if I'm all right?" she asked, narrowing her eyes at me in typical Andy fashion. I felt so happy seeing her conscious and hearing her talk like that.

"Anybody who knocks themselves out needs checking over at hospital," Sue told her with a smile.

"I don't remember anything about it," Andy said frowning. "I just remember jogging round, deep in my daydreams ... and the next thing I knew was when I woke up a minute ago."

When we got to the hospital Andy was transferred to a trolley and whipped away to be looked at. Mum and Dominique (Andy's mum) arrived at the hospital at the same time as each other. Mum immediately came flying over to me and gave me a very gentle hug, which got tighter as she realized that I wasn't hurt.

"Andy's regained consciousness, Dominique, and she's absolutely fine," I told Andy's mum straight away.

Dominique nodded but didn't say anything. I didn't think she was capable of speaking. Her eyes, which are very big anyway, looked enormous, set in her small, pinched face. Mr Blundell came back from the vending machine at that point with two cups of tea. I introduced him to Mum and Dominique, then a nurse came to take Dominique off to see Andy, and Mr Blundell went for another cup of tea for Mum.

Mum wanted to know how Mr Blundell fitted into the story, as all she knew from Mrs Pemberley was that Andy had knocked herself out on the rec. I began to explain about the man, without saying that I'd seen him before. But I needn't have worried. All Mum wanted to know was whether or not the man had harmed me in any way. I assured her that he hadn't touched me and she let out a huge sigh of relief and didn't ask me any more questions, except about Andy.

A few minutes later we were standing at Andy's bedside. Dominique was sitting on the bed, holding Andy's hand.

"They're keeping her in overnight," Dominique told Mum in a worried voice. "Apparently they do that when there's a head injury involved."

"I'll be all right, Mum," said Andy, smiling brightly for her mum's benefit, but poor Dominique still looked eaten up with worry.

"It's just to be absolutely sure, Mrs Sorrell," the nurse smiled.

"Oh, no!" Andy suddenly groaned.

We all pressed forward.

"What?" I asked first.

"The cross-country. I presume I won't be able to do it?" Andy asked, despondently.

"If it's tomorrow we would definitely advise against it," the nurse answered, firmly.

"It's all up to you then, Fen," Andy said.

"Oh, what a drag," I replied, feeling totally depressed about it. "I had this dream last night that we beat everybody and came into the funnel at the end at exactly the same time, and were declared the joint winners."

"You'll just have to imagine I'm with you when you win," Andy grinned.

"You're joking. There's no way I could ever win. I'll just try not to let the team down. And I'll come and see you the moment it's finished."

"Yes, that would be great. I'll be at home by then."

Andy lifted one limp hand out of the bed and we shook hands very gently.

"Deal!" we said at exactly the same time.

Isn't it strange how time blurs our emotions? When I was at the height of my terror, staring into the eyes of that man and praying desperately for help, I'd resolved there and then to make my big confession to Jan straight away, even before the magic evening. And hang the consequences!

And yet, here I was, under two hours later, at home, safe and sound with my family, and my resolution had gone completely down the drain. Well, not completely, because I still intended to make the confession, but not till after the magic evening. After all, it couldn't possibly do any harm just working that one evening. There was no way that that man would dare even to think about coming back to the café after all that had happened.

The police had just been arriving at the hospital as we were going. The doctor had said it was fine for Andy to give a statement. She would probably confirm what I had already told them about seeing the man in the café. Other than that she wouldn't be able to say anything more about him, so I guessed that that would be the end of it. All the same, I figured the man would probably have been unnerved by the sudden appearance of Mr Blundell. No, I knew he wouldn't dare come back to the café again.

Mum had asked me on the way home whether or not I'd ever seen the man before and I admitted to having seen him in the café, but I didn't say that it had been on Wednesday evening when I'd first seen him, or that he'd been interested in how old I was. I certainly didn't tell her how I'd lied to him about my age and why I'd done that.

The following morning I woke up feeling no different from usual, until slowly my brain moved up through the gears and I remembered the awful events of the previous day, followed by the big event of this afternoon. I felt nervous, but excited and determined to do well.

Mr Cobb had been very disappointed to hear that Andy wasn't going to be well enough to run, but he'd said he'd find a replacement for her. I guessed he was probably thinking that our team hadn't a hope now, and that made me more determined than ever to grit my teeth and run like I'd never run before.

Afterwards I would go straight to Andy's place and tell her all about it. The minibus would go right past her house so I didn't even need to go home first. I'd already phoned the hospital and found out that Andy was fine. I'd also phoned Tash and told her the whole story of yesterday.

Her gasps had got bigger and bigger until in the end I'd had to hold the phone away from my ear, because I'd thought her next gasp might explode my eardrum! She'd wished me megatons of luck, and said she'd see me at seven o'clock for the magic show, then we'd rung off.

Mum was going to come and support me at the cross-country, but then Emmy had had a temperature which had got worse overnight, so Mum had had to stay at home to look after her. Dad had a work meeting, which happened from time to time on a Saturday. They were both feeling guilty about not being able to come and support me, but I assured them I really didn't mind, because not many people had their parents there watching.

The minibus arrived at Lowerden Forest School, where the cross-country was taking place, at twelve o'clock.

"Right," said Mr Cobb, "go and get changed, girls, then we'll walk the course together so that you can get an idea of what you're in for."

We didn't walk the whole course because that would take too long and might wear us out, so we kept short-cutting and just walked the most important parts. Some teams don't even bother to do that, because it isn't necessary as far as knowing where to run was concerned. It was true that this particular route was complicated, though, with roped off sections appearing every so often, or big metal arrows stuck into the ground to show you where to go when it wasn't too obvious.

Mr Cobb was excellent at giving us tips. He said we had to stay together as a group as much as possible. "Fen will set the pace and you others do your best to keep up with her," he instructed the year-nine girls, which made me feel very proud, but also slightly anxious, in case it got on their nerves having a year-eight girl to set the pace.

"I hope I can do it," I said quickly. "I'm not like Andy, you know."

Two of the year nines immediately started to encourage me and tell me to think positive, then I'd be the fastest person there. I was happy that they had such confidence in me, but at the same time I didn't particularly like the weight of the responsibility I felt, with everybody pinning their hopes on me.

"This bit's very muddy," Mr Cobb was saying, "so keep to the left just here... Then over here you can practically cut the corner off. There'll be one or two stewards from Lowerden Forest dotted about the course when you're actually running, so there shouldn't be any risk of you taking a wrong turning," he told us. "Oh, here is an excellent overtaking place. You won't need this, Fen, because you'll already be ahead," he grinned.

"I doubt it," I retorted.

"Course you will," the year-nine girls smiled. I didn't have any fears about whether or not I was popular with them any more. They'd been really kind to me, and I was beginning to feel the determination running through my veins with the adrenalin.

Before our race, there was the race for girls of twelve and under. Then it was our race, then one for boys of fourteen and under. The twelve and under race was only two miles long but the other two races were both three miles long. Usually on a three-mile race the person who came in first would take about twenty-four minutes and the last stragglers might take up to about thirty-five minutes.

There was always a funnel at the end of a cross-country race. That meant that the very last twenty metres or so of the course was roped off so that you could only run single file and no over-taking was allowed. Then each person was given a position.

It was important for each member of the team to do fairly well because the positions were added together. It was no good having four of your runners coming in at say second, third, fifth and sixth, if the other four runners were placed in the fifties or sixties. For our competition today, there were ten schools competing so that meant eighty runners.

"You must get out there in front right from the word go," Mr Cobb kept stressing. "Remember your training. Sprint the first hundred metres."

We all nodded nervously, then we stopped talking because the starting pistol had gone off for the race before ours.

The great horde of girls surged forward. It was fascinating to watch the expressions on their faces. Some looked strong and determined, others looked strained, and others looked completely at ease, as though they were setting off on a short jog to post a letter or something.

As the great throng spread out into a clump followed by a straggly line, the crowd began to split up too, making their way to the various good watching-points. Some people stayed put and resumed their conversations. My gaze drifted round and I caught sight of a girl I knew from Woodman's.

"Hi, Andrea," I called out.

She looked round to see where the voice was coming from, then smiled and waved. "Hi, Fen. Are you running in the under-fourteens?"

"Yeah. Are you?"

"Yeah."

"Good luck."

"Thanks. Same to you."

My gaze moved round further, and there standing not two metres from Andrea was

Matthew. His eyes met mine and narrowed knowingly. I blushed like mad, partly because of seeing him when I hadn't been expecting it, but mainly because now he'd sussed me. He knew for sure that I'd been lying about my age. I felt such a fool. I was dying to go over to him and explain everything, but there was no way I could do that.

I could see he was cross, very cross. I didn't like that hard look on his face. It somehow didn't go with Matthew. A couple of metres away from him that aggravating Barry was taking everything in – me, my age, Matthew, his reaction, everything. I turned my back on them both and asked Mr Cobb when we'd be starting.

"About fifteen minutes now, Fen. So keep warm. Do some gentle jogging. I want you on top form."

He grinned at me and I tried to grin back but it wasn't easy.

Chapter 5

We were all lined up at the top of the field ready to go. I was taut like a spring, rocking backwards and forwards very, very gently. The talking amongst the competitors had died down to a whisper, and then fizzled away into silence as we waited.

Bang! Off we went. There was lots of shouting from spectators and teachers. The spectators mainly consisted of pupils from Lowerden Forest, although there were a few parents there too. I could hear Mr Cobb's voice amongst the others.

"Go on, Fen! Go for it!"

He didn't have to tell me. I was going! My legs felt as though I could do anything with them. My arms pumped hard, and already I could feel myself getting ahead.

Some teachers made the mistake of telling the

runners to pace themselves and conserve their energy, but Mr Cobb always told us to run our hardest right from the word go, across the field, because towards the end of the field the running area narrowed and narrowed until it was just a track with only occasional places for overtaking. So it was important to get into a good position right from the start, because your chances of doing well were much slimmer otherwise.

I'd done it! I was actually in the lead as the field narrowed into the track which went through the woods. The run was entirely through the woods from this point onwards, and in places it was very thick wood as well. The woods merged into Lowerden Forest, from which the school took its name, and part of the course touched on the forest.

A feeling of confidence and determination took me sailing along. Andy would have been proud of me. I passed a steward with a yellow coat on, and he smiled and congratulated me on running fast.

"My goodness, you've got a wriggle on, haven't you! Keep up the good work!"

I managed to side-track the muddy bit and took a left turn where the roped off bit made sure I followed the right route. It was another overcast and slightly misty day, and I found myself looking forward to seeing another steward in a yellow coat.

The section of the course that touched on the forest was drawing nearer, and as far as I could tell I'd built up quite a good lead. There didn't seem to be a soul for miles around. I kept my eyes on the ground to make sure I didn't miss any route directions, because my sense of direction wasn't all that good, and this course was definitely the most complicated I'd ever run.

A little way ahead I'd spotted one of those arrows that stick up out of the ground like a mini-signpost. It was pointing to my right, and it's a good job it was there because this was a part of the course we hadn't walked. I glanced behind me but there was still no one in sight.

A twig cracked very near by and some leaves rustled. I looked round to see who it was, but it must have been a squirrel or some other little animal, so I ran on hard to catch up the valuable seconds I'd wasted. This track was a bit flatter than the one I'd just been on, and it was a relief to be able to run so easily without having to worry about slippery or rocky ground underfoot. I felt exhilarated.

After about two minutes the track narrowed and descended and the trees around me suddenly seemed to be very dense. My eyes searched the ground for signs, but there just weren't any. Then the track split and I didn't know which fork to take.

Come on, Fen, think, I told myself firmly.

It was then that the first feelings of unease crept over me as I realized that I'd somehow managed to get myself in the forest. But part of the course was supposed to touch on the forest, wasn't it? Yes, but…

I looked slowly all round me. There was no sound but the rustling of leaves high up in the trees and my heart banging against my ribs as I puffed and panted.

Did I miss an arrow? I wondered with gathering anxiety. *I must have done.*

Perhaps if I ran back up the narrow track I'd run down a few minutes before, I'd see someone coming up behind me? I was on the point of doing this when I thought again. I couldn't have gone wrong. I'd been looking out for arrows all the way, and I'd definitely not been mistaken about the last one. It was indicating the very route I'd taken. These arrows were made of heavy metal and sunk well into the ground. There was no way the wind could alter their direction.

No, I'd just better pull myself together and get running before I lost my lead by dithering about. It must be a left here, then I'd soon get back on the track, even if I *had* gone slightly wrong.

I ran determinedly along, pushing any worries I'd had about going the wrong way right to the back of my mind. The track wriggled and turned until I felt dizzy with the effort of trying to hold on to some feeling of orientation. Slowly I was realizing something. There was no way I could be on the right track... I had to admit it. I was lost.

My running slowed to a jog, then to a walk and finally to a standstill. I stared around me in dismay. I'd stopped kidding myself that everything was fine. It was obvious that everything wasn't. I was alone in a vast forest and I had absolutely no idea at all how to get back to the real track. I looked at my watch and realized with a shock that thirty-four minutes had gone by since we'd all set off. That's when I sat down on a thick branch that trailed over the ground, and cried.

I only cried for about three seconds, though, because I'm not the crying type. These were tears of frustration that after all my efforts, I'd totally screwed up and let Mr Cobb and the rest of my team down. I thought about the year-nine girls. How they would laugh behind my back now! I could just hear them talking to their friends on Monday morning. "That's the last time I run with a pathetic year-eight girl. She's supposed to be so great, and what does she do! Goes the wrong way! Talk about thick!"

I put my head in my hands, then immediately sat up straight again with the realization that I'd got to do something. At least I had to *try* and get back, to make it easier for the search party that would no doubt be setting off at that very moment.

The best bet would be to jog back in the direction I'd come from, and this I started to do, but after a few minutes the track disappeared and I found myself in the middle of hundreds of tall, tightly packed conifers, bracken underfoot, shades of darkness all around. My heart was really racing then, even though I was standing perfectly still.

My eyes flew round wildly then I began to run – anywhere, just anywhere – in a blind panic. I had to find some kind of main track before it got dark, because not only would a main track lead back to civilization, but mainly because the depths of the forest would be dark long before everywhere else.

I ran and ran, stumbling and slipping and grazing my hands as I reached out to grasp hold of branches to balance myself, and scratching my legs on the undergrowth. Then suddenly I rolled on my ankle and felt a stab of pain as I fell down. The whole weight of my body had fallen against an uprooted tree stump and the sudden force against it made it move. I lost my footing and slithered painfully into the gaping hole it had left. Then as soon as my hands eased their pressure off the stump, it fell back into place with me stuck beneath it.

Using every ounce of strength I possessed, I tried to shove the tree stump out of the way, but my legs were clamped down and my arms weren't strong enough without something to push against. It was only brute force that allowed me to free one of my legs, the one with the throbbing ankle. I found a foothold, but the pain that seered through my ankle was so great, I couldn't put any pressure on it at all. With a feeling of utter helplessness and fear I flopped back like a rag doll, my face pressed into the dirt. And this time I did cry – hot tears that seeped into the forest floor.

After a minute I stopped abruptly because I suddenly realized that I had been staring into the eyes of a rabbit! Practically its whole body was hidden by bracken which covered the thick, gnarled roots of the massive tree trunk. I must have been looking at it for some time, but because it hadn't moved, I hadn't realized what it was.

"Hello, fella," I said softly, reaching out a hand towards it. Still it didn't move, so with a great effort I tried to heave myself out of my trap. My hand was almost touching the rabbit now but still it didn't move. Its eyes blinked at me, and it turned its head and wriggled urgently, but couldn't get away.

"I don't know who's the more scared, you or me, Rabbit," I told him quietly. He did another scuffle in a vain attempt to free himself. "We're both trapped, I'm afraid," I went on, "and you're scared of me, I know. But you do have one advantage over me, fella. You're quite at home here. The forest is what you're used to, but me – I'm a total stranger. So you've got to help me to stop being afraid of this place, and in return I'll set you free, when someone comes to find me. OK?"

The rabbit blinked and I tried again to move just another five centimetres so that I could touch him, but it was no use. I couldn't. This time though the rabbit didn't try to get away. He stayed quite still, then his head went down and rested between his front paws, like a sleepy dog.

"You're not scared of me any more, are you, Rabbit?" I said, softly.

He regarded me gravely.

"I can't keep calling you Rabbit, can I? What shall I call you? I know – Bracken. After all, you're surrounded by the stuff, aren't you? There's one thing I've got to warn you about, Bracken, and this is it. Any time now we're going to hear voices, because the search party must be coming closer – at least I hope it is – so listen, Bracken, don't be alarmed when I let out the biggest holler of my life, will you? I've got to do it, otherwise the search party won't know where to look, you see…"

Bracken raised his head and lowered it again.

"Got that all right, Bracken?" I checked, because at that moment in my life he was the best little creature on earth. He was my friend, and he was keeping his part of the bargain, because I wasn't half as scared as I had been, now I'd got someone to talk to.

"Don't worry, Bracken. You'll soon be free. You'll soon…"

I shut up abruptly because I'd heard something. It was only very faint, but I was sure I hadn't been mistaken. I held my breath and waited. There it was again – a man's voice calling my name!

"This is it, Bracken! Block your ears!" Then I did the loudest scream I could muster. "Over here!!!"

Bracken flinched and the undergrowth around him rustled a little.

"Ssh, listen," I told him seriously.

We listened, but I realized it was hopeless. I was stuck in a hole down a slope, and I wasn't even facing the right way for my voice to carry.

I waited to hear if they would call again, and after a moment, sure enough, I heard the voice again. It was a powerful voice, a voice used to shouting, but it was coming from such an awfully long way away. I tilted my head back and sideways so my yell might carry a bit further.

"Over here!!!"

I thought my vocal chords were going to snap I was working them so hard. But there was still no answer, no footsteps pounding over to me. I waited and waited ... and waited, and then flopped back again because there were no more voices, not even faint ones. The search party was moving further away from me, not closer.

The face of my watch was very dim when I tried to decipher the time. Four-thirty. *Four-thirty!* I should have been on the minibus, heading towards Andy's for a quick "Hello" before the magic evening.

I'd completely forgotten about the magic evening. Oh, what a mess. What a stupid, stupid mess.

Then Bracken made a noise. I'd never heard a rabbit make a noise before. In fact, I didn't think rabbits *could* make noises, but I was sure I hadn't imagined it. Bracken had made a noise!

"Sorry, Bracken," I whispered, reaching my hand out towards him. "Am I ignoring you? Is that what you're trying to tell me?" Again, I used all my strength to make my arm reach the teeniest bit further so I could touch him. I managed another centimetre but that was positively the furthest I could reach.

Then something amazing happened. I felt Bracken's soft nose rub against my fingertips. I definitely hadn't moved at all. It was Bracken who had moved towards me. He had wriggled himself just close enough for my fingers to touch him. I stroked the tip of his nose and the tips of his paws, and felt a tiny little bit of courage raising my crushed spirits. Good old Bracken. I didn't know what I would have done without him.

Twenty minutes later, my head shot up as I heard my name being called again. This time I even recognized the voice. It was Mr Cobb. I gathered all my strength again, took a deep breath and yelled back. "I'm here, Mr Cobb! I'm here!!!"

"Keep shouting, Fen," he yelled back, and I did, until I was hoarse. But I didn't care about that. A bubble of happiness was rising up inside me. Mr Cobb was getting closer and closer; I was about to be rescued. I was at last going to get out of this horrible ordeal. Then I saw him above me. He was sliding and slithering down the bank beside the tree stump.

"Thank goodness we've found you. You're safe now, Fen... Are you hurt?"

"Only my ankle."

"Don't try to move too quickly. You'll be terribly stiff after all that running, especially now you will have cooled right down."

A woman came slithering down the bank next, then another man. I didn't know either of them.

"Thank goodness you're safe," the woman also said, as she put her arm round me and gave me a quick hug, even though she was a complete stranger. I didn't speak. I didn't know what to say.

The two men heaved and grunted and finally shifted the tree stump. Immediately I tried to get up, but my legs wouldn't support my weight, and like a new-born pony's they crumpled beneath me. I took a sharp breath as I felt the pain in my ankle.

"Don't try to move, Fen. We'll carry you," Mr Cobb said.

"It's OK. I'll be all right in a second." I tried again, but more cautiously this time, and holding tightly on to the woman's arm.

"This is Mr and Mrs Massey, by the way, Fen. They both teach at Lowerden Forest."

I smiled and looked at them properly. They were probably in their mid-fifties and looked very gentle and kind.

"I'm the school medical officer, actually, Fen, and my husband teaches geography," smiled Mrs Massey. "Careful now. Lean your weight on me. I can take it."

Mr Cobb was supporting me on the other side and I could feel myself unstiffening. The only problem was my ankle. I turned it gently, then very cautiously put a little bit of weight on it, then a little bit more. It wasn't as bad as I'd thought it was going to be. Mrs Massey reckoned the rest had probably done it good.

"Let's get you back then, Fen. It's getting dark," Mr Cobb said.

"Oh, hang on!" I exclaimed suddenly, remembering little Bracken. "There's this rabbit that's trapped. I've been talking to him the whole time I've been waiting for someone to come and find me."

The three adults watched as I crouched down by the big old tree trunk.

"Here he is," I announced, turning to Mr Cobb, who was looking at me as though I was slightly mad.

"I don't believe it," Mrs Massey breathed slowly as she gripped her husband's arm, and looked as though she'd stumbled upon some buried treasure. "Look! It's Terry!"

"My goodness, so it is!" exclaimed Mr Massey. They were both staring incredulously at Bracken, but a second later they turned as if in slow motion to each other and let out a sort of helpless, mirthless laugh.

"Not that easy to get rid of, Terry old chap, are you?" said Mr Massey, bending down and giving Bracken the kind of look you'd give a little child who'd done something naughty but so sweet that you didn't have the heart to be cross. I stood up because my ankle was hurting me, and Mrs

Massey, presumably seeing the puzzled look on my face, explained Bracken was actually Terry, the school rabbit who'd just escaped for the third time.

"So how did Brack ... Terry come to be in the forest?" I asked.

"Well, two days ago we noticed that the door to his hutch was open, and when we examined the catch we saw that it was loose. It must have slipped down or something. Of course, we felt terrible, especially as it's happened before. Maybe having a school rabbit isn't such a good idea..."

"And here he is," I finished off for her, bending down to give Bracken another stroke.

"Would a pet rabbit survive in the wild?" I then asked carefully.

"Well, he's not making a very good job of it so far," commented Mr Cobb, who was not surprisingly beginning to shuffle impatiently from foot to foot.

I was aware of Mr and Mrs Massey giving each other subtle questioning looks, and reaching the very decision I was willing them to reach.

Mr Massey coughed. "Um ... we were wondering... As you've obviously got quite attached to the old fella, would you like to keep him?" he asked me.

"If your parents agree, of course," added Mrs Massey.

My heart leapt. "Yes, yes, that would be excellent," I told them. "Mum and Dad wouldn't mind, I'm sure."

So Mr and Mrs Massey released Bracken's back legs which were caught up under two long pieces of tree root that wove tightly in and out of the ground. Then Mrs Massey gently picked him up and put him in my arms, where surprisingly he snuggled down quite happily. He felt so soft and sweet and cuddly. And he was all mine!

"Right, shall we make tracks then?" Mr Cobb said, still trying not to sound impatient. "The rest of the search party will be wanting to hear the good news that you're safe, and so will your parents and friends."

It wasn't easy walking with a rabbit in my arms but somehow I managed. The first bit was the worst because of having to climb back up the slope. I put up with the pain in my ankle because I so much wanted to keep Bracken. He didn't wriggle about at all.

Mr Cobb had given me his tracksuit top to wear because I was beginning to feel the cold. Surprisingly, until that point I hadn't felt at all cold because luckily I'd been trapped in a sheltered place. It was easier carrying Bracken inside the tracksuit top. As we made our way back I asked about the race, embarrassing though it was.

"Which school won, Mr Cobb?"

"Heatherfield," he answered. "We weren't given a position because of only having seven runners. But Jayne and Gemma did well – fifth and sixth, and the others were all between tenth and twentieth."

"We would have won, wouldn't we?" I said, softly.

"If you'd have come first we would have won. But it's not your fault, Fen. It's just one of those things. The important thing is that you're safe."

I slowly began to explain, then, why I had finished up in the forest. I told Mr Cobb and the Masseys that there was no doubt in my mind that the flag was pointing the way I went.

Mr Cobb frowned and looked perplexed, then raised his eyebrows at Mr and Mrs Massey.

"We'll certainly look into it, Fen," Mr Massey said, "but there just doesn't seem to be an explanation."

"Unless someone moved the flag," said Mrs Massey, as though she was thinking aloud.

"But why would anyone do that?" Mr Cobb asked me. "You haven't got any enemies or over-keen rivals, have you, Fen?"

He had asked me the question almost jokingly and I had answered with a grin, "Not that I know of." But he'd got me thinking, and for a while none of us spoke. I guess we were all turning over the possibilities in our minds.

My own personal thoughts had settled on one name – Matthew. I kept on seeing that hard look on his face. A little argument had broken out inside my head…

He wouldn't do a thing like that.

Why not?

Because if anyone had seen him he would have been in deep trouble.

He took a risk. It paid off.

But why would he do that?

Because he hates you.

No, he doesn't. Why should he?

Because you made him look a fool in front of Barry and the others.

Just because I gave him the impression I was sixteen…

He thought you were taking the mickey, pretending to be interested in him, then giving him the big put-down.

We were approaching the place where the flag had directed me into the forest.

"This is the flag you meant, isn't it?" asked Mr Massey.

I nodded and stared at it. It was pointing the other way from the way I had run.

"Someone's changed it round," I said. "I know I didn't get it wrong."

"And you've no idea of anyone who might have got it in for you?" Mr Cobb asked me again.

I hesitated, then said that I didn't, because I had nothing at all to go on, and I didn't want to look a fool if Mr Massey started accusing Matthew. I knew it was obvious that Matthew wouldn't admit it, after all. And nobody could prove it. He had got back at me in the very cleverest possible way.

I was treated like a long-lost arctic explorer when we arrived at the school field. The year-nine girls from my team all flew round me and demanded to know every detail of my absence. Mr Cobb went to phone Mum to explain what had happened.

The girls were more interested in Bracken poking out of the top of Mr Cobb's tracksuit that I was still wearing than the thought of me, all alone, trapped in a dark forest. But Bracken wasn't interested in them. He hid himself further and further inside the tracksuit top whenever any of them tried to stroke him. The other four members of the search party had returned and were obviously really relieved to see me.

Most of the other schools had gone. There were just the pupils from our school, the host school and Woodman's still there. The last few members and supporters of the Woodman's team were making for their school minibus. The rest were already in it. I could see Matthew and Barry sauntering along.

"What did she say?" I asked Mr Cobb, who had come back from phoning Mum and was trying to round us all up.

"She was obviously very relieved to hear from me, and very concerned to check that you were all still in one piece… Oh and she said, 'Don't worry about the café. Natasha is working until you get there.' She sends her love."

"Oh, right. Er, Mr Cobb? I shan't be a sec. I just want to…"

My voice trailed off as I limped towards Matthew. My ankle was much better but still hurt. I couldn't really tell Mr Cobb why I wanted to speak to a boy from Woodman's, but I guessed he'd reach his own conclusions and probably think he was my boyfriend or something.

"Matthew," I called out.

He turned round, and so did Barry. Barry was grinning as usual but Matthew wore that same dark, threatening expression, which quite suddenly made me feel really angry. How dare he cause me so much fear? *And* pain.

"Did you turn that flag round, Matthew?" I snapped at him, coming straight to the point.

"Course he didn't," answered Barry, chewing gum and hopping from foot to foot as though he was incapable of keeping still. His face broke into a sort of drunken-looking grin as he caught sight of Bracken, or at least noticed a bit of fur poking out from inside Mr Cobb's tracksuit top.

"Brought back a nice souvenir from the forest then, have we?"

"Shut up, Barry," said Matthew. Then he turned to me. "Are you OK?"

I was completely taken aback by the sudden change in his voice and expression. The black look had gone and in its place was a look of concern.

"Course she's not," Barry answered for me in his infuriating way. "She's totally cracked. She can't even follow a simple cross-country route, can she? Come on, Matthew, let's get going." With that Barry turned away.

Matthew looked as though he wanted to say something but changed his mind, and, a second later, he too turned on his heel and off they went.

Feeling rather foolish and very angry, I turned back to join Mr Cobb and the others.

Very clever, Matthew, I thought bitterly, because I was more certain than ever now that it was he who had made sure that I wouldn't win, to pay me back for making a fool out of him at the café. He'd even got that revolting Barry boy in on his secret.

Right, Matthew, I'll get you back. You may think we're quits, but you went too far, you did. So just you wait!

Chapter 6

The magic evening was going really well. Because there were so many people there Jan had told Tash she could carry on working even when I'd arrived and started work. It wasn't the kind of evening that people of our age would normally go to, but working together in that atmosphere was really great, particularly as I no longer had any fears of that awful man suddenly appearing. The grown-ups were being very noisy, laughing far more loudly than was necessary, and shouting more and more to make themselves heard, as everyone else was so noisy.

Andy was completely better, but wasn't coming to the magic evening. Leah had gone round to Andy's to keep her company. Luce and Jaimini had been persuaded by Mum to come round to our place and babysit Rachel, Emmy and Bracken, as Mum and Dad were here at the magic evening. Both Jaimini and Luce had known all about what had happened to me, even before I'd got home, because of Mr Cobb's phone call to Mum. Mum had phoned Tash, and Tash had phoned the others.

Jaimini had called in to see Andy, who had given her a card to give to me. I thought it was so sweet of Andy to send me a card. It should have been the other way round, really. The card had a picture of a fat, furry rabbit that was winking on the front. Mum had laughed at how brilliantly appropriate and comical it was. Then I had gone upstairs to read what Andy had written...

Bad luck about the cross-country. We'll get even somehow. Have a great evening – your last one. Hope you're feeling brave about tomorrow. Phone me when you've talked to Jan.

Loads of love

Andy.

The card had been all about me – not one single thing about her, and yet we'd scarcely had the chance to talk about what happened on the rec. Andy was so selfless, and the events of yesterday evening seemed so far away because of all that happened since.

At the magic evening I was very much the centre of attention for a while. With everybody talking to me and making such a fuss of me, I gradually began to realize just how much had happened to me in such a short time. Here, in this buzzy café atmosphere, the events of the afternoon seemed like a dream somehow. Jan, Mum and Tash all wanted to know who could possibly have been so stupid and horrible as to turn the flag round to prevent Cableden from winning. And Jan was obviously preoccupied about this for some time.

"I hope they conduct a proper inquiry into it," she said vehemently.

"Absolutely," Mum agreed with feeling, and as I looked from one to the other, I thought how alike they were. They both have sharp bone structure and their eyes are their strongest feature, because they can make them glint with anger then change to a real doe-eyed look far more quickly and obviously than most people can.

Just then they were both looking at me with the same intense frown, and I knew they were wondering if I had any bright ideas about who the phantom flag-remover might be. I had actually already decided it was better to keep shtum on that subject.

Of course I'd confided in Tash and she thought I ought to just forget about it, and get on with my life as though it had never happened. I wasn't so sure I agreed with her though.

Bracken, as I said, was safely at home in the

hutch that used to house our guinea pigs. The guinea pigs had died about eight weeks before, within about a week of each other, and we had all been too upset to replace them with any others. The hutch was quite big and Luce had brought a bag of hay with her. She and Jaimini had assured me they would pick some grass and give it to Bracken, along with a couple of carrots and plenty of loving attention, so I wasn't worried about him from that point of view.

My only anxiety for him was that he might feel trapped again, having had the whole big forest as his playground and being back in this small space. Dad had already agreed to make a big run for him so he could graze in the garden and only go in his hutch at night times where it would be a nice cosy place to sleep. I secretly hoped that when the weather got better I'd be able to let him loose in the back garden, as long as I was with him, of course.

When I'd told Dad about Bracken being trapped in the forest, he had just looked rather thoughtful and commented that perhaps we ought to take him to the vets to get him checked over.

I was thinking about Bracken as I was serving what Jan calls nibbles. Kevin had made quiches, vol-au-vents, Parma ham wrapped round asparagus tips, and various other tasty titbits.

There was also a choice of Cheddar, Brie or paté ploughman's on the menu.

To drink there were all the usual soft drinks, but most people had white or red wine, and there were some cans of lager as well as some low alcohol white wine, which was quite popular.

My dad was really enjoying himself. He was in a great mood, making a joke out of everything. He loves joking, does Dad, but he does have another more serious side to him. I watched him joking with Raj, the magic man, and pretending he was a magician too. Raj and Dad were laughing heartily and kept slapping each other on the back, much to the amusement of the adults around them.

Every so often Dad glanced up and gave me a broad wink. He used to do this a lot when I was younger, especially during things like school plays and concerts. It always amused him – *and* half the audience, I expect – when I winked back. Since then it's become a sort of standing joke, that no matter what the circumstances, if Dad winks at me, I have to wink back. Sometimes it can be really embarrassing, but so far I've always managed to keep it up.

Tash and I were worked off our feet, though the work seemed to be in patches. Whenever we had a quiet time, though, we took turns to go and hover by a table where Raj was doing a trick and watch him. It was a very casual evening because Raj didn't do his show from the front, he just went round the room from table to table and spent a few minutes at each table, doing his magic.

His tricks were absolutely brilliant. For example, at one point, I watched him pour some salt into a woman's upturned left palm. Then he told her to close her fingers up over the salt and also to close up her other hand, and turn her hands over. He then instructed her to slowly cross her hands over each other and back again a couple of times. While she was doing this he simply tapped both her hands very gently once or twice.

"Right, and now for the moment of truth," he said, with a cheeky grin all round. "Turn your hands over and open them up," he told the woman. This she did, and everyone gasped in amazement because her right hand had salt in it, and the left hand was completely empty! Of course, we all burst into applause.

Raj moved on to another table and I went back to work, even though there wasn't a great deal to do. I cleared a couple of tables, then was on the point of telling Tash to have a break and watch Raj for a bit, when I saw a man get up and go over to Jan. He looked very serious and bent his head confidentially towards Jan as he talked.

I could tell he was talking about Tash because

he kept looking at her. So I sidled up a little closer to Jan until I was just behind her back, and clearly heard the man say, "All the same, it's well past seven o'clock. I'm afraid it's simply illegal."

My heart began to thud, especially when Jan gestured to Mum to come over. I wiped some glasses and listened in, feeling sick.

"This gentleman has just been pointing out to me that it's against the law for the girls to work after seven o'clock in the evening. I thought you said you'd cleared that with the LEA, Dee? In fact, I distinctly remember you told me that they said it was no problem because of the girls working so infrequently."

I went cold all over when Jan said that, and my heart raced at the thought of what Mum was about to reply. I could feel the net closing in on me and there was absolutely nothing I could do, except stand there, drying glasses.

"Hang on a sec, Jan. It was *you* who told *me* that. I remember it clearly, because Trev and I were worried about that until you said it was all right... Ah, now, hold on a sec..."

As Mum slowed down and started frowning in concentration, thinking back, trying to recall exactly what *did* happen, I broke once again into a cold sweat and awaited my inevitable fate. I killed the time – short though it was – wiping glasses with such intensity that I'm surprised I didn't break at least one. Jan's and Mum's wide eyes fixed on each other as realization dawned on them both at precisely the same moment. They even spoke together very slowly, as though they shared one voice between the two of them.

"It was Fen…"

Then their eyes flew round the room looking for me, before they both swished round and clamped their steady gaze on my red face. The man had been following all this with interest as though it were a good sitcom or something.

"Fen," Mum started, her voice razor sharp and dangerously low, "you lied to me."

Jan cut in with the same accusing tone. "And you also lied to me."

"I'm, I'm sorry."

At this point the man left us. I expect he realized that the embarrassing bit was about to come.

"Why, Fen?" Mum asked, her eyes pleading with me to give her some kind of explanation that might, by some miracle, excuse my behaviour, and make everything all right.

"Because … it had all been such a great idea, to have the café opening one evening a week, then suddenly I remembered that we weren't really supposed to work after seven o'clock, and I knew that you and Jan would think about that straight away … and it seemed such a small thing to stop us from working, when it was only going to be once every six weeks. So before I could help it, I just found myself telling you both a lie."

"You can't go taking the law into your own hands like that, Fen. You just can't!" said Jan, crossly.

"I never thought you could act so deceitfully," Mum added, making me feel unbearably guilty.

"I was going to confess it all tomorrow, Jan. Honestly."

Tash appeared at that moment.

"Confess what?"

"You know," I mumbled.

"Oh," was all Tash could manage.

"So you're in on this too, are you?" Mum said, turning her angry eyes on poor Tash.

"No Mum, it's not Tash's fault. The moment she knew about it she told me to come clean. I was just waiting for this evening to be over, because I knew Jan was really excited about it, and I didn't want to let her down."

"Well, I've had enough!" Jan suddenly snapped in a cold fury. "You're suspended, Fen. I don't believe this rubbish about telling me the truth tomorrow."

"But..."

"Don't give me any 'Buts'. I can't believe anything you say any more. As from now you're suspended from the café rota altogether until further notice. You could have got me into really big trouble. In fact, you probably have. I don't know who that man is. I've yet to find out, but I only hope he's an ordinary member of the public, and not someone who works for the LEA or something."

I took off my apron and so did Tash, and we went and sat in the kitchen on our own until the end of the evening when Mum and Dad were ready to go.

Mum had taken our place and helped Jan out for the last part of the evening. Tash and I felt like naughty outcasts and sat miserably in our enforced isolation. Tash was kind. She could easily have said, "If only you'd done what we told you to do, none of this would have happened." But she didn't say a word of rebuke and I was grateful to her.

After a long silence she eventually said, "Don't worry, we'll get you out of this somehow. The biggest problem is that Jan didn't believe you when you said you were going to own up tomorrow."

"I know," I answered, miserably.

I felt even more downhearted when I thought about Dad. Mum would no doubt have told him about his deceitful daughter, because she would have had to explain why Tash and I had suddenly disappeared off the face of the earth.

As I was contemplating this, the kitchen door

opened and in he came. Jan had been in and out several times, but hadn't even looked at us. When Dad came in I thought it was Jan again.

"We're ready to go, you two," he said quietly, every trace of his previous jocular mood gone.

We dropped Tash off at her house, then Dad took Luce and Jaimini straight back. I didn't get the chance to tell them about the evening, though they must have noticed the atmosphere between me and Mum and Dad. We just had a quiet word about Bracken, who had apparently been asleep all evening, then off they went, agreeing to meet up the following day at Tash's place. (Tash and I had arranged this at the café.)

Then I flopped into bed without saying "Night" to Mum, because I didn't want to hear her cold voice when she answered.

The following day we all sat round in Tash's bedroom and talked and talked about the magic evening, the rec, the man and the cross-country. Mr Cobb had phoned me and Andy to tell us that there was to be a rerun of the under-fourteens girls cross-country race the following Saturday, because Mr Cobb himself had put in an official complaint. This time there were to be stewards positioned at regular intervals.

Just talking about the events of the cross-country took us ages and ages, but by the time we'd discussed the magic evening, and all that happened on Friday evening as well, over two hours had gone by.

I think all six of us still felt a small lingering fear about the man on the rec. I thought I probably wouldn't relax completely until I knew he'd been caught, although we weren't really sure if the police were even looking for him. Andy said that she thought they probably weren't, because they'd taken such brief statements from us.

As far as my suspension from the café was concerned, the others were sympathetic, but not perhaps as sympathetic as they would have been if I'd been sensible and taken their advice right from the start.

"I expect Jan'll come round soon," Leah had offered.

"Well, I hope so, otherwise it's goodbye Café Club for me," I replied, rather bitterly.

"I'm sure Leah's right," Tash added.

I thought she probably was, but all the same I had the feeling that things would never really be the same again because I had deceived Jan, and she would feel she couldn't trust me.

"At least you've got your lovely rabbit," Luce said, launching into a rapt description of how absolutely cute Bracken was for the benefit of the three who hadn't seen him yet.

"Even that's got a downside," I said, sadly.

"What do you mean, a downside?"

"I mean I think there may be something the matter with Bracken. He's acting strangely. It's as though he's pining or something. He lets me pick him up, and he does snuggle in, but he doesn't want to eat much at all."

"Perhaps you ought to take him to the vet's," Luce suggested.

"That's what Dad said."

"What does your mum say?" asked Jaimini.

"Not a lot at the moment," I replied, with a long-suffering smile.

"Oh, dear, is she still upset about last night?"

"You're not kidding. She's going about with a really tight-lipped expression all the time. I don't know how on earth I'm ever going to get back into Mum's or Jan's good books. I've really messed it up this time."

"Look on the bright side, Fen," said Luce, with a wicked grin. "It's nothing compared to the trouble I get myself in."

The others laughed, but I just didn't feel like joining in.

"So when *are* you going to take Bracken to the vet's?" asked Tash, trying to change the subject.

"Dad reckons we should leave it a little while longer, and if he's still refusing his food, take him then."

I must have been looking really glum because

Tash suddenly jumped up and called downstairs to her little sister, Peta. Peta is very entertaining, but we usually go out of our way to make sure she's not in the same room with us because she goes totally hyper and makes it impossible for us to even talk. I was quite surprised that Tash had called for her to come up, surprised and touched, because it was obviously for my benefit.

Peta scrambled upstairs in next to no time and came thundering into Tash's bedroom, shouting maniacally and doing a wild dance as though she belonged to some little-known Pygmy tribe or something. Peta often went right over the top when she was excited about something, and the reason she was excited this time was because Tash's mum had strictly forbidden her to come and disturb us in Tash's bedroom, even though Peta had been desperate to come up and join in with "those big girls", and now all of a sudden, she was actually being *invited* in!

"Calm down, Peta," Tash instructed with a serious attempt at a frown which she couldn't keep up for more than about two seconds, before dissolving into helpless giggles along with the rest of us.

This only had the effect of making Peta even more excited. She started singing while pretending to hold a microphone in front of her, her tiny little hips gyrating round in the funniest imitation we'd ever seen of pop dancing.

It took less than half a minute for me to forget my problems and be reduced to a helpless quivering wreck just like all the others.

"I knew my little sister would do the trick," laughed Tash. "She never fails."

"I never fail, I never fail!" screeched Peta ecstatically, clapping her hands to one side then the other. "I clever fail, I clever nail…" Her lyrics were becoming more and more ridiculous by the second. "And I bang the nail," she carried on at the top of her voice, as she went round giving us all a bash on the head.

"Be careful, Peta. You're getting too rough. You're going to hurt someone," Tash warned her sternly.

"All right, big sillies, I'll go and bash Danny on the head."

"Now you're just being stupid," Tash rebuked Peta crossly. "Nobody's laughing now, are they?"

Of course when Tash said that we all had to pretend not to be laughing but it wasn't easy, and we finished up shaking with suppressed giggles, while our eyes watered.

Tash's mum, Helen, came in at that point and scooped Peta up.

"Time to go, I think," she said, rolling her eyes at us, as Peta bashed Helen's back and carried on shouting, "Bang the nail! Bang the nail!"

As soon as she'd gone we all collapsed, then gradually pulled ourselves together. It was Andy who spoke the first sensible words.

"Who's working tomorrow?" she asked.

"Me," said Luce.

It had been Leah on Saturday before the magic show, and nothing out of the ordinary happened.

"Let's all go to the café after school tomorrow," Andy proposed.

"I'm not sure I'll be welcome," I said hesitantly.

"Yes, you will. You've got to face the music," Andy argued. "Just act perfectly pleasantly towards Jan, and after a bit that'll make her feel really guilty and childish for being cold and unfriendly."

"I'm not sure..." I began.

"No arguments," Luce interrupted, holding her hands up in front of her.

"OK," I agreed reluctantly. "I'll come." And everyone cheered!

Chapter 7

So there we were on Monday – five of us sitting round a table with Luce on duty. Luce loves taking orders and serving people. She's had one or two mishaps in her time, but they haven't reduced her enthusiasm at all!

Most of the work we have to do is washing up or other chores in the kitchen. When we first started work at the café, Jan had a rule that we weren't allowed to serve, but she pretty soon relaxed and started gradually giving us more responsibility.

On this particular Monday, we'd been in the café for about fifteen minutes and hadn't even caught a glimpse of Luce. Mark had taken our orders and brought our drinks and buttered toast. We didn't usually have anything to eat, because we were nearly always skint, but this day I think we felt the need for a bit of sustenance.

Whenever Becky isn't working, a boy called Mark works. It sounds stupid calling him a boy, because he's quite tall and seems more like a man than a boy, but he's only seventeen. He works part-time at the café, and part-time in one or two other places too, to earn money while he's studying the Martial Arts. He's ace at karate, is Mark!

"Buttered toast all round," he announced grandly as he put it down in front us. "Celebrating something, girls? You don't usually eat at this time of day."

"We're trying to keep out the cold," I said, nodding in Jan's direction, with a sour look on my face to show Mark that I was not exactly flavour of the month as far as Jan was concerned.

"Aha, so my instincts were right!" said Mark. "Has Luce done something to upset Jan because it's a long time since Jan has been *this* uncommunicative."

"No, it's my fault," I quickly corrected Mark. "And it's a long story," I added, because I couldn't be bothered to go through it all again. "Poor Luce."

"Yeah, poor old Luce," agreed Jaimini. "She's so often in trouble for things which *are* her fault, it seems totally unfair that she even gets into trouble when it's not her fault."

Jaimini wasn't deliberately trying to make me

feel bad, I knew, but that was the effect her little speech had on me.

"I shouldn't worry about it if I were you," Mark said. "She'll come round. She always does."

With that, he disappeared and I sighed for the millionth time, thinking that perhaps I ought to go home, then the atmosphere might clear. It was just as I was thinking that that the door opened and in walked Matthew with Andrea and another girl.

All three of them immediately looked over in our direction, but only Andrea smiled and waved. I'd never set eyes on the other girl before. Andy knew Andrea too because we'd seen her at various inter-school sporting events, but the others had never seen her.

"Who's that with Matthew?" asked Leah.

"Andrea Stewart," replied Andy. "She goes to Woodman's too."

"Which one's Andrea?" asked Jaimini.

"The taller one. I don't know who the other girl is."

"Do you think Matthew's trying to tell you something?" Andy asked with a giggle. I wasn't amused. I still felt very mixed up as far as Matthew was concerned.

At that point Luce appeared and squatted down beside me, looking rather huffy.

"Who does he think he is? Hugh Grant?" she asked rather snappily.

We all smiled at Luce's view of her "gorgeous specimen" with two girls.

"How's Jan?" I asked her, with an apologetic look on my face. "We gather from Mark that she's taking out her temper on everyone in sight."

"That's about right," said Luce, rolling her eyes. "I'd better go. I don't want her coming over here barking instructions at me."

"I'm going in a sec," I told her. "Things'll probably improve then."

Luce went back to work and I reached into my bag for my purse. I was about to put the money on the table when Andrea appeared at my side.

"Hi, Fen," she said cheerfully. "Hi, Andy." She glanced round the table and gave everyone a quick smile so I introduced her to Tash, Leah and Jaimini, but although she smiled at them I could tell she was wanting to get the introductions over with so she could talk to me.

"Matthew sent me over actually," she began, sounding a bit embarrassed.

"I know he's your friend, Andrea," I said, wanting to put the score straight right from the word go, "and I know he wasn't too happy with me the last time he came in here, but that was nothing compared to what he made me go through at that cross-country. So you can tell Matthew to get lost!"

I had felt my temper mounting as I'd been making my little speech, and the last bit of it came out rather more harshly than I'd intended. I stood up and grabbed my bag.

"Bye, you lot. I'll see you tomorrow."

They didn't answer. They were looking at Andrea to see what effect my hard words had had on her.

"That's why he wants to talk to you, Fen. You see, it wasn't him."

I stopped in my tracks to consider this. She had certainly managed to shock me, but that was all.

"Sorry Andrea, I know you want to defend him, but I'm afraid I can't buy that one."

"You mean you don't believe me?" Andrea asked me, in a shocked voice.

"No, I mean I don't believe him," I answered.

"Well, you would if you'd only just come to our table for a couple of minutes before you go. Please, Fen."

"Go on, Fen," whispered Tash.

"Who's that other girl?" I asked cautiously.

"Carly. She's Matthew's sister, and my best friend."

"Oh … right."

"Matthew refused to come in here with me, just in case people thought we were going out together, so he dragged his sister along too."

"But why?"

"Because he knew you'd be in here and he wanted to explain things."

"Go on, Fen," Tash repeated.

"Oh, all right," I agreed finally, with yet another sigh. I couldn't help noticing the relief on Matthew's face as I approached their table with Andrea.

"Hi, I'm Carly," said his sister, with a lovely big smile. She was really pretty when she smiled, and I liked her straight away.

"I'm Fen, but I expect you know that," I said, which I instantly regretted saying because it sounded like I thought I was something special.

She didn't answer, just nodded. Then the smile disappeared and she looked at her brother as if to say, "Go on then. Get on with it."

Matthew leaned forward.

"Listen Fen, I'm really sorry about the cross-country. The thing is, I'd never do anything like that. I just wouldn't."

"Oh sure! Belief!" I said in a hard sarcastic voice.

Matthew looked at Andrea for help.

"He didn't, Fen," she said. "The reason I know that for sure is that I heard Matthew talking to Whittaker just before your race."

"Who's Whittaker?"

"He's one of those boys who watched me make a fool of myself in here the other day," Matthew answered, sounding decidedly hacked off. "The one who you spoke to after the cross-country. You know – Barry."

"Oh, that irritating little nerd, yeah. Look, I couldn't help what happened in the café the other day," I defended myself.

"So why pretend you're sixteen when you're not?" Matthew came back at me.

"It's a complicated story and I can't be bothered to explain it right now, but it was to do with the man who was sitting at that table," I said pointing to the corner table.

"Oh, *him*," said Matthew, that awful sneer reappearing on his face.

"Can we get back to the point?" said Carly, tossing an exasperated look at her brother.

"Right," Andrea continued, "as I was saying, I overheard Barry and Matthew talking. Barry had noticed you standing with the Cableden team, Fen, and he immediately turned to Matthew and said loudly, 'If she's sixteen, I'm a Martian.' Matthew had already worked that one out, because he'd heard me ask you if you were running in the under-fourteens, and he heard your answer too…"

Andrea paused and looked at me, but I didn't say anything because she hadn't told me a single thing to convince me of Matthew's innocence yet.

"Fen, I didn't know anything about what had

happened in the café," Andrea went on. "All I knew was that when I looked at Matthew a moment after I'd spoken to you about the under-fourteens, he had a face like thunder and I couldn't work out why. That's what made me move closer to him. I was going to ask him what was up. But I never quite got round to that, because he and Barry were talking by then. The trouble was I missed the very beginning of their conversation so the rest of it didn't make an awful lot of sense to me, but this was roughly what I heard... If you want me to tell you?"

I nodded and she started talking very quickly and precisely.

"Barry said, 'You're an idiot if you daren't even do that.'

"Matthew said, 'I'd be an idiot if I did, more like.'

"Barry said, 'I thought you wanted to pay her back.'

"Matthew said, 'I do, but not like that.'

"Barry said, 'Well, if you won't, I will.'

"Matthew said, 'You wouldn't dare.'

"Barry said, 'Oh no? Just watch me then.'

"Matthew said, 'If you do that you'll be really living up to your nickname...'"

"Dimwhittaker," Carly whispered to me quickly, before Andrea continued without a break.

"Barry didn't answer Matthew. He just stomped off with a face like thunder."

Andrea stopped abruptly and leant back in her chair. There was a silence that seemed to go on for ever because I was weighing up all she'd just told me.

"But I don't understand why you're even friends with Barry," I said to Matthew.

"No, sometimes I don't either," Matthew replied, frankly. "Actually, I suppose I'm not really friends with him. He's just one of the crowd I hang about with. The trouble with Barry is that he likes to be where the action is. Then he tries to get in on it, but somehow he always gets it wrong and goes too far. He can be a great laugh a lot of the time, but other times he can really get on your nerves. And right now I can't stand him."

Matthew stopped abruptly and I turned my attention to Carly again.

"It wasn't Matthew who turned the flag round, you see," she said slowly, looking me straight in the eyes. "I know he can be a pain at times – and believe me I *do* know, after all I live with him. But he wouldn't do a thing like that."

Again there was a silence, but briefer this time.

"I don't think Barry had any idea of the trouble he would cause. He just wanted to prevent you from winning," Matthew explained. "Straight after he'd turned the flag round, he came over to tell me. He was really proud of himself, and he told the boys in his gang, too. Of course, they'd never dare to split on him because in some ways he's like the big leader, you know."

I nodded, and Matthew carried on.

"Barry was boasting about how he'd hidden behind a tree and couldn't believe his luck when you came running along way ahead of the others. He said it didn't take two seconds to move the flag and get back behind the tree. Apparently he thought you'd seen him, because you hesitated before following the direction of the arrow. As soon as you'd gone, he nipped back and turned it round so it was pointing in the right direction."

"So why didn't you report him?" I asked, in my same unforgiving tone, even though I felt much less harshly towards Matthew by then.

"I dunno, because I'm a coward I suppose," Matthew answered frankly, with a shrug.

I think that was the moment I changed my mind towards Matthew and started to like him again. He wasn't pretending to be anything other than what he was. He was so straightforward and honest.

Andrea interrupted my thoughts and gave me a shock all in one go.

"*I* reported him," she said.

"*You* reported him?" I repeated, incredulously.

"Yes, but nobody believed me. I sent an

anonymous note to the headmaster."

"You see, even *she's* a coward," Carly grinned.

"It just seemed stupid to get involved," Andrea explained. "I only wanted to see justice done," she added.

"And was justice done?" I asked. "Did Barry get punished?"

All three of them shifted about in their seats then, and I had to repeat my question.

"Barry's very clever at getting out of trouble," explained Matthew, slowly.

"What do you mean?"

"He just denied it. He looked and sounded completely innocent, and said he didn't know what on earth the Head was on about."

"Did you hear him talking to the Head then?" I asked.

"No. Barry was called into the Head's study, but as usual he came boasting back to his mates, telling us the whole story word for word. I'm not one of his mates any more, though."

"Why not?"

"Thanks to my little sister, I suppose."

"What!"

"Carly had a go at him," Andrea explained.

"*You* did?" I asked Carly in amazement, because she looked so young to be having a go at a year-eight boy.

Andrea must have read my mind. "Carly's a

year seven, she just looks much younger," she explained.

"I could hear Barry boasting away to the others, because they were all in the corridor and I was waiting outside the loos for Andrea," Carly explained, "so I just called out, 'You'll get caught one day, Dimwitty. Just you wait!'"

I gasped. Carly was certainly very brave to confront someone like Barry in that way.

"Did he think *you* wrote the note to the Head when you said that?" I asked, wide-eyed.

"I don't think Barry even knows there *was* a note," Andrea answered. "The Head's very discreet."

"So what did he say when you said you bet he'd get caught one day?" I asked, turning back to Carly.

"He just laughed and said, 'No I won't, because it's impossible ever to prove it was me.' Then he suddenly turned nasty, and said, 'I hope you haven't been telling tales about me, little clever Carly,' and I didn't even bother to answer him. Well, that must have made him assume it *was* me who had dobbed on him, because his expression turned really horrible and he said, 'Two can play at that game, you know. If you can dob on me, I can dob on your brother, can't I?'"

"So, did he?"

"We're not sure," Andrea answered. "Matthew

hasn't been summoned to see the Head yet, but if I know Barry Whittaker he'll do his level best to land Matthew in the biggest trouble he can. He can't stand Carly because she stands up to him, and sometimes manages to make him look a fool in front of his band of followers."

"What a rat!" I commented, fiercely. Then I turned to Matthew. "We've got to pay him back."

"The thing that really bugs me," Matthew said, "is that he's right. It *is* impossible to actually prove that it was him who turned the flag round."

"I'll get the others to help me think about this one," I said, thoughtfully. "Between us we're sure to come up with something."

"We ought to be going, Matthew," said Andrea, putting the money for her Coke on the table.

"Yeah, we'd better," agreed Carly, looking at her watch.

"What's your phone number?" I asked, quickly.

Matthew scribbled it down on the corner of a napkin which I stuffed into my pocket.

"I'll call you when we've worked out a plan," I told him.

"Can I take your phone number as well, just in case you forget?" he asked, a bit sheepishly, which made my spirits leap up and dance. I told him my number, and he said he'd remember it, then off they went, calling out "Bye" to everyone on my table.

As soon as I'd sat down with the others, they urged me to tell them what he'd said. So I gave them a blow-by-blow account of the whole conversation, and they listened intently to every word.

"The rat!" said Andy, when I'd finished.

"That's what I said," I told her.

"How are we going to get him back?" Jaimini asked.

"I don't know."

"Why don't we all go home," Tash suggested, "and have a really good think, then compare notes tomorrow and see what we've come up with."

"Yeah, good idea," I said.

"What about Luce?" Leah asked.

"I'll phone her later and tell her the whole story," Jaimini offered.

At that moment Luce reappeared, looking slightly flushed. "Blimey, it's hot in the kitchen," she said, parking her bottom on half of Jaimini's chair. "I've just tried to tackle Jan," she added, in a tired voice.

"I hope you haven't made matters worse," Jaimini said, immediately.

"No, but then again I haven't made them any better," Luce admitted. "I just told her that you really were very repentant, Fen, and she said she didn't particularly want to talk about it, because she was still feeling hurt that you were trying to pull the wool over her eyes."

"Did you tell her that Fen was fully intending to come clean yesterday, but she didn't want to spoil the magic evening by owning up before it?" Tash asked.

"Yes I told her, but she flatly refused to believe me."

"We'll just leave her alone, and I expect she'll come round soon. Like Mark says, she always does."

With that we parted ways, Jaimini calling to Luce that she'd phone her later.

When I got home Mum was still acting coolly towards me.

"How's Bracken?" I asked.

"I think he's all right," she answered, sounding just a little less cold than she had been of late. "He's probably just naturally a docile rabbit."

I went out into the garden and took him out of his hutch. He cuddled into me straight away without trying to get away, and I talked to him for a few minutes before putting him back. It was true, he wasn't exactly the liveliest rabbit I'd ever come across.

When I'd done my homework, I came down and ate with the rest of the family. Dad was back to his old jokey self, but somehow it didn't quite extend to me. He tickled Emmy, then tried to get Rachel to look the other way so he could nick her chicken nuggets, but I had the feeling I was just outside of the family fun. Mum, to give her her due, was trying to draw me into the conversation, so she'd obviously thawed out a little.

Back upstairs I continued with homework until Rachel appeared with the phone. "It's for you," she said, handing it to me.

"Hi, Fen, it's Andy."

"Hi, Andy."

"Leah and I were chatting on the phone and we got talking about Barry and we wondered whether or not Matthew and the girls could pay him back by finding out what his favourite thing is – you know, something at school that's really important to him – and mess it up in some way. Like if he'd got something excellent on a computer, they could erase it."

"Yes," I said, hesitantly.

"Or if PE was his favourite subject they could hide his kit."

"Yes…" I wasn't entirely sure why I was hesitating. "Give me one more idea, Andy."

"Well, let me see – if Barry had spent ages on an important piece of homework, Matthew could accidentally spill something on it."

"You mean, so Barry knew it was him?"

"No, no of course not. That would get

Matthew into trouble."

"Exactly." I had worked out what the flaw in the suggestion was. "Surely we want Barry to know that it was Matthew who ruined his work. Otherwise none of us will have the satisfaction of knowing that Barry realizes we've managed to get our own back on him."

Now it was Andy who was hesitating. "I see what you mean. The trouble is that even if Barry *did* know it was Matthew, that's not really what we're trying to achieve, is it?"

"What do you mean?"

"Well, it's *you*, not Matthew, who wants to pay Barry back, isn't it?"

"Yes, you're right," I said, a bit despondently.

"I've got an idea," Andy said, a hint of excitement creeping into her voice. "Matthew could leave a clue! Like, say he was trying to spoil a piece of Barry's homework, he could write the word FEN right across it. After all, Barry couldn't prove that it was Matthew who did it, just because it said Fen on it! He'd be putting Barry in exactly the same position as the one Barry put you in."

"Yes, that sounds brilliant," I agreed enthusiastically. "I'll phone Matthew right away."

I'd no sooner rang off, though, than the phone rang again. This time it was Luce.

"Hi, Fen. Jaimini's been filling me in on that creep Barry, and this is what I thought of…"

I was about to tell her that Andy and I had already decided on something, but she didn't give me the chance – just launched into her plan.

"I reckon that he needs to be made to look a fool in front of his whole class. Or, even better, if his whole tutor group was really hacked off with him because he'd destroyed their chances in some inter-tutor group competition or something. We haven't worked out the fine details yet, because we need to talk to Matthew first."

I told Luce that I thought her plan sounded really good, and then explained what Andy had come up with, and we agreed that I ought to contact Matthew right away because we'd thought of several alternatives by then, but couldn't decide which was the best one without his help.

Again I was just about to tap in the number when the phone rang. This time – I might have guessed – it was Tash! Her mind had been working along exactly the same lines as the rest of us, but a little more strongly, which was surprising for Tash. I expect that was because Tash was more upset than the others about what I'd suffered in the forest. She said, why didn't we set up something really mean like stealing something from another pupil and planting it on Barry. Yes, I thought wickedly, that would really show him.

Finally, I did get to phone Matthew and we had a long discussion about all the different suggestions. As we were talking, we came up with one or two other good plans too, and finally decided on the four best ones, which Matthew, Carly and Andrea would carry out between them.

According to Matthew the best day for one of the plans would be Friday, because Barry, Matthew and Andrea all had double games in the afternoon. These were the four plans.

The first one was up to Matthew and Andrea to carry out. Apparently Barry and Matthew were in the same tutor group and they were doing a play for assembly, but because the play was so popular with all the pupils, the teacher had turned it into a full-scale production which their tutor group were going to perform for the rest of the school.

Barry had the main part and was therefore allowed to keep the glossy mastercopy of the script, whereas the rest of the class had A4 photocopied sheets. The teacher had apparently warned Barry of the importance of not losing the script.

Matthew was going to sneak the script out of Barry's bag and give it to Andrea to hide somewhere. They would return it after a couple of days when Barry had been made to suffer.

Tash's suggestion had been taken up for the second plan. We hadn't decided exactly what should be stolen, but we thought it might be taken from a teacher, which would be even worse. Carly was going to do that one, and Matthew was going to plant the stolen item on Barry.

The third plan was to vandalize Barry's tech project. Apparently, in woodwork, they'd all been making puppets, and Barry was particularly pleased with his. The puppets were about to be judged. Matthew said that the whole class was sick of the way that Barry was going round telling everyone that his puppet would easily win. Well – not the whole class – but all except Barry's little gang. Andrea was going to get a pair of scissors and make large cuts in the puppet's jacket, trousers and shirt.

And last but not least, the fourth plan. This was also going to be the last of the four to be carried out. This would be the moment that Barry would realize who had been behind all the tricks, but he would be absolutely powerless to do anything about it.

When the boys went off for PE on Thursday afternoon, Andrea would be doing outdoor activities with the rest of the girls. Apparently it would be very easy for Andrea to ask if she could go to the loo, and even if she didn't return for five minutes, the PE teacher wouldn't really register how long she'd been away.

Andrea was going to find Barry's kitbag in the

boys' changing room, get his locker key from it, unlock his locker, and write *I love Fen* in Tipp-Ex across the front of his French exercise book. It was French straight after games, last lesson of the day, and this would be the final straw as far as Barry was concerned.

Matthew and I could scarcely contain ourselves on the phone when we thought with great satisfaction about finally getting our revenge on Barry.

"Be careful though, Matthew, won't you? And tell Carly and Andrea to be careful, too. It would be disastrous if any of the plans went wrong and you got into trouble."

"Don't worry, we'll be fine," Matthew said confidently. "We'll meet you in the café after school on Friday and tell you all about it."

I went to bed that night with the feeling that, though I couldn't yet see the light at the end of the tunnel, I could sense that it was approaching. I was still very afraid that Jan might never forgive me for deceiving her, and I'd be out of the Café Club for good. But at least Mum was acting a little more friendly, and Barry was soon to get what he deserved.

Chapter 8

The next three days were very long, frustrating ones. We were all dying for Friday to come so we could hear how Barry had suffered.

Jan had thawed out quite a lot and was now managing to say "Hello" to me when she saw me in the café. She was acting completely normally towards the others, but refusing to discuss with them the question of whether or not she might forgive me, and allow me to go back to work. Mark was still advising me to hang on in there and just hope that eventually she would give in.

I should have been working on Thursday but Tash did it instead. Afterwards Tash said that she'd told Jan she was going to give the money to me. She was hoping that that would make Jan feel guilty, but it simply seemed to irritate her, apparently.

"What you do with your wages is none of my business," Jan had said with her hands on her hips and her head tilted to one side.

There were two high spots to the week, however. One was that Bracken seemed to be much better. He had gradually started to eat his food and move around a bit more. We borrowed a huge rabbit run from someone who Tash's mum knew. This meant that every day Bracken could go out and graze in the garden. Dad reckoned that he must have just taken a little while to settle in with us. He was certainly fine now.

The other good thing that happened was that the police phoned Mum to tell her that a man answering the same description as the man I'd seen in the café, and then on the rec, had been arrested in a place called Bewbury which was miles away.

A woman police constable came round to our house with a photo so I could say if it was the same man who had frightened me at the rec. It was. It made me shudder just seeing the picture of him. The police constable told me and Mum that he'd been charged with attempted abduction.

I felt an immediate feeling of relief for two reasons. One, because he'd been caught and so I didn't have to give him another thought and two, because I had realized by then how lucky I had been to have escaped unharmed that fateful day.

The other important thing about the week was that Andy and I worked hard training in break times and lunch hours. I knew I wasn't running quite as well as I had been the previous week. I couldn't have said why that was even if Mr Cobb had asked me. But he was careful not to push me by asking too many questions. Perhaps he thought I was still affected by my interesting little detour the previous week. He did ask about my ankle though, and I was able to tell him that it was completely better.

It was true that my ordeal was still affecting me, but all the same I wanted Mr Cobb to push me more, because it was frustrating not being able to run as well as I knew I could. Andy, on the other hand, was going from strength to strength.

Every time I got depressed because she was running so much faster than me, she'd turn to me and say, "Fen, what's the matter with you? Come on, you're supposed to be the ambitious one. Where's all that fiery determination of yours?"

I couldn't give her an answer to that one, because I simply didn't know. It was probably just the fact that I'd run my very, very best the last time and I didn't think I could possibly repeat it.

Eventually Friday came and we all trooped down to the café after school. Jaimini was on duty. Tash had had to nip home first and collect Peta. She was supposed to be babysitting because

Danny wasn't at home, Tash's mum was at work, and Peta wasn't well enough to go to nursery school that day. A neighbour was looking after her till Tash got home from school, but as soon as the neighbour had gone, Tash bundled Peta into her buggy.

"It's not as though she's really ill or anything," Tash justified herself. "She's just very snuffly and subdued. A little ride in the buggy'll do her good. And anyway, I'm not missing what Matthew has to say for anything!" she added, with a very Luce-like grin!

Matthew still hadn't appeared at the café when Tash turned up with a very quiet Peta, along with a bag of colouring books and sticker books and things to keep Peta amused.

When Matthew, Andrea and Carly eventually arrived, we beckoned excitedly to them to come and join us. We had reserved the table next to ours so that we'd all be close enough to hear what Matthew had to say. Funnily enough, neither Matthew nor the other two looked particularly excited. In fact, come to think of it, they looked downright glum.

"How did it go?" I asked, still hanging on to a thread of excitement, but knowing in my heart that I was going to be disappointed.

"Useless," replied Matthew and Andrea at the same time. Carly said nothing.

"So what went wrong?" Luce asked. "Surely something must have gone right?"

"No, nothing," replied Carly. "It was all a total waste of time."

"What do you mean? Tell us what happened," I insisted.

"Right, plan number one," began Matthew, sounding extremely cynical. "Getting the script from Barry and giving it to Andrea was no problem at all. Andrea had decided it was best not to leave it in her bag, or anywhere where she or any of us might be connected with its disappearance."

"So," interrupted Andrea, "I left it in the library. To be precise I left it in one particularly boring section of the library that no one ever takes books out of. In fact, the books in that section are caked with dust, they're so rarely taken out…"

"But wasn't it just our luck," interrupted Carly, taking up the story, "that some keen sixth former happened to want a book on harmony and counterpoint, and discovered the missing script!"

"Being a very diligent and public-spirited sixth former," Matthew continued, sounding more cynical than ever, "he took the script along to the staffroom, where our very grateful form tutor thanked him profusely and returned the script to Barry, saying 'And don't lose it again'."

"And that's all?" asked Leah, looking as though

someone had short-changed her by a long way.

"'Fraid so," Andrea sighed. The other two leaned back in their chairs with their arms folded, looking so similar with their dark heads tilted to one side, and sour expressions on their good-looking faces.

"So what about the second plan?" asked Tash.

"Plan number two," began Carly, "totally back-fired on us."

"Why?" we all asked, leaning forwards.

"Because on Wednesday I managed to take Mrs Reynolds's very expensive Parker pen from her open bag, when she was talking to someone and no one was watching me. I gave it to Matthew so he could put it in Barry's pencil case."

"So far so good." Matthew took up the story. "We took the pen home with us on Wednesday after school, and, sure enough, on Thursday morning in assembly Mrs Reynolds made an announcement that she had somehow mislaid her very precious Parker pen, and asked if we could all be extra vigilant and return the pen to her if we happened to come across it lying around the school. The Headmaster then added that he hoped the pen had not been stolen, and that if it was discovered that this had been the case, the person concerned would be severely dealt with.

"So I planted the pen in Barry's pencil case, and watched carefully when it came to the next lesson. I was sitting just behind him and could clearly see him open his pencil case. He took the pen out very slowly. I couldn't see his face but I could just imagine him looking totally horrified to see it there.

"Then the next thing I knew, Barry had leapt across the room to one of the front corners where the waste-paper bin was. The maths teacher was looking totally gob-smacked and said, 'Barry, what *are* you doing? Get back to your place at once.' And Barry, who had hidden the pen up his sleeve, pretended to pick something up from behind the bin, then held the pen up triumphantly to the maths teacher.

" 'Look, sir,' he cried excitedly, 'I think this must be Mrs Reynolds's pen! It was just sticking out a tiny bit, or I wouldn't have seen it!'

" 'Oh, well done, Barry,' said the beaming maths teacher, and to cut a long story short, Mrs Reynolds gave Barry five pounds as a reward!"

"Oh, no!" we all wailed together. It was unbelievable that two out of four plans had gone so horribly wrong.

"What about the third plan then? Tell us the worst," Andy said.

"Plan number three," began Andrea, in a very flat voice, "I carried out yesterday after school when the tech block was pretty deserted. I sneaked into the workshop and found all the puppets on display. They were named and it didn't take me a minute to find Barry's.

"Personally I reckoned it didn't stand a chance of winning because there were some really brilliant ones there. But just to make absolutely sure, I got some good sharp scissors and made loads of snips in the trousers and a few in the jacket so that the puppet looked really tatty.

"I felt pretty horrible doing it, I can tell you, but I just kept telling myself how scared you must have felt all alone in that forest, and how frustrating it must have been to have had the chance of winning the competition taken away from you like that. Then I sneaked out and went home.

"This morning, the results of the competition were announced, and the prizes were given out in assembly. Guess who won? Jammy Barry! And do you know why? Because the judge thought that making the puppet into a ragamuffin was a stroke of pure genius!

"Barry spent the whole of the rest of the day gloating to anyone who'd listen to him. He pretended to his mates that he'd gone back into the tech block at the end of school and added the artistic snips on a sudden stroke of inspiration. I saw his face in assembly, though. It was an absolute picture. I've never seen anyone look so totally baffled while desperately trying not to."

"As the day went on," Matthew continued, "I was aware of Barry watching me at odd moments. I didn't give anything away, mainly because I didn't want to give him the satisfaction of knowing I'd played right into his hands."

"You may as well finish us off," I said. "What went wrong with plan number four?"

The others looked exactly as I felt, I noticed. They were all resting an elbow on the table and cupping their heads in their hands.

"Plan number four," announced Andrea, sarcastically, "went like this. I got Barry's locker key from his kitbag without any problem, and took his French exercise book out. I looked for his Tipp-Ex pen in his pencil case, but he hadn't got one and I didn't want to use an ordinary pen. So I decided I'd squeeze a little blob of ink from one of his cartridges on to the front of his book, then smear it into the words *I LOVE FEN*, only with a heart instead of the word love. I was going to do the smearing with his fountain pen.

"Unfortunately, his cartridge let out more than a blob, and when I tried to smear it, it didn't look like anything at all. It just looked like a big, blotchy, disgusting mess.

"Anyway, I decided that that couldn't be helped. At least I was confident that Barry would get a good telling-off, and possibly even a detention."

"So what happened?" asked Leah, turning to Matthew.

"Well, there we were at the beginning of French, all getting our books out. Again I made a special point of sitting just behind and a little to the right of Barry so I could watch what happened when he saw his book. It looked an absolute mess. Andrea had certainly made a thorough job of it. But Barry just stuck his hand up and said, 'Sir, I'm afraid something terrible has happened. My cartridge has leaked all over the front cover of my French exercise book. I don't know how it could have happened.'

"The French teacher asked Barry to hold it up, which Barry did, only to be told, in a very sympathetic voice, that it was bad luck, and that the best thing would be to go home and cover it with brown paper."

"Oh, great!" I concluded, miserably.

The others said similar sarcastic things and then we all sympathized with Matthew and the girls and thanked them for trying.

All through these stories I had completely forgotten about Peta who was sitting on Tash's knee and sticking stickers in a book. She suddenly announced, "Silly ole fing!" as though she'd been following the whole story perfectly.

"You're being a very good girl, Peta," Tash praised her little sister. This had the effect of making Peta stick her stickers in even more slowly and carefully as though the compliment had given her renewed enthusiasm. I noticed that every so often she glanced round to see if anyone was watching her. Peta certainly likes being the centre of attention! Looking at her stickers I thought how clever it was to make a man and a woman out of straightforward shapes like triangles and circles.

"So what do we do now?" asked Andy, bringing my attention back.

"I reckon we forget it," said Tash. "It all sounds too risky for Matthew, Carly and Andrea."

"I'll tell you something," Matthew threw in, "I think Barry might have the suspicion that I'm in league with you, Fen, and we're both involved in some kind of revenge campaign."

"What makes you think that?" I asked. "Has Barry actually said anything to you?"

"No, it's just the way I keep catching him looking at me. And also, the French teacher took him on one side at the end of the lesson, and I deliberately listened in. He was asking Barry if he had any idea how the book might have got into that state. Barry replied that he couldn't work it out. Then the French teacher asked him if there was any way that someone else might have done it on purpose, and did he have any enemies?

"I watched Barry carefully. He was on the point of saying something, then abruptly changed his mind and said no, he didn't have any enemies, and he thought that one of his cartridges must have just leaked. If you ask *me*, Barry suddenly realized what the French teacher was getting at."

"What do you mean?" asked Luce.

"Well, if Barry admitted to having enemies, he'd have to say who, and that would lead the teacher into making connections with the cross-country. You never know. So Barry was actually protecting himself by going along with the leaky cartridge theory."

Luce nodded slowly, and as she was nodding my stomach turned over, because into the café walked Barry and a few of his mates.

"It's Barry!" I hissed, and quick as a flash we all turned into our own conversations and nobody looked up at all for the next minute or so. We didn't want Barry to see Matthew talking to us or he'd definitely put two and two together. It would be totally humiliating for Matthew and me, if Barry mocked us for failing in our revenge.

After a minute or so, we heard him call out, "Watcha Matthew," and Matthew looked up innocently and called back, "Watcha Barry," then carried on talking to Andrea and Carly with a pretty bored sort of take-it-or-leave-it look on his face.

"The toerag!" said Leah, which was quite strong for Leah.

"I hate him," added Tash.

"Hey," I said slowly, my whole body beginning to tingle because a great plan was forming in my brain, and all because I'd been staring at Peta's sticker book to give Barry the impression that I was nothing to do with Matthew.

"What?" asked Leah, tugging at my sleeve. And I told them all my plan as quickly as I could. It involved the café loos. You have to go through a door to get to them, which leads into a very short passage with the phone on the right and the doors to the loos on the left.

"Right," I said, when everyone understood. "We've got to get Matthew to go to the toilet."

I tried to catch Carly's eye without Barry or his friends noticing.

"Also," I went on, "somebody needs to go and fill Jaimini in, as she's quite an important part of the plan."

We all looked round for Jaimini, but she was nowhere to be seen. It seemed strange looking round the café. I'd been so involved in the "Barry" story, that I'd forgotten where I was for a little while there. I'd had the same feeling that you can sometimes get when you go out of the cinema in a sort of daze, and face the real world outside.

"I'll go and have a word with Jaimini," Luce offered, getting up to go to the kitchen. So I went back to trying to attract Carly's attention, which I succeeded in doing almost immediately.

Meanwhile Andy had scribbled the following message on a bit of paper:

When Fen gives you a nod, go to the cake counter with Carly and pretend to be deciding which one to have. All part of an ace plan – you'll see.

Andy slipped the note to Carly who was nearest, and jerked her head in Matthew's direction to indicate that it was for him. Carly discreetly passed it to Matthew, who read it and gave the tiniest of nods, then pretended to be reading something on the wall behind my head, though I presume he was making sure he was ready for my nod.

Barry, meanwhile, was telling his friends loudly about what a lucky week he was having, what with earning five pounds and winning a cup. Then they were discussing us lot. It was impossible to hear exactly what they were saying, but it was perfectly obvious that Barry was trying to make us feel uncomfortable. We just caught the odd snippet and the odd snigger, like "Yeah, bet she dyes it. All girls dye their hair, cause they're really vain, see."

As soon as I saw Jaimini emerge from the kitchen, I nodded at Matthew, and he and Carly got up and went over to the cake counter.

"Did you manage to explain it to Jaimini?" I checked with Luce as she came back and sat down with us again.

"Yes, she's thoroughly briefed," Luce reported, enjoying the drama.

Jaimini was pretending to talk to Matthew about the choice of cakes, and how much they cost, but in actual fact she was telling him to go to the loo, and then go straight over to Barry and tell him to go and have a look in the gents' because somebody had written something really funny on the inside of one of the toilet doors.

Andy, meanwhile, had slipped off to the loo with a black felt-pen. It was one of those thick, heavy ones. She also had two stickers from Peta's book, the ones I had spotted of a man and a woman. With very little time it was vital that she worked quickly, and this is what she had to do.

Her first task was to go into the ladies' loo and write in big bold letters *I STOPPED FEN WINNING. SERVES HER RIGHT. B W.*

Next she had to drop the pen in the waste-paper bin, go out of the loo and take the sticker of the man and stick it firmly over the picture of the woman on the door to the ladies'. She then had to stick the picture of the woman over the picture of the man on the door to the gents'.

All this had to be carried out extremely quickly

because of course the plan would be ruined if any of the other customers really did want to go to the loo.

As soon as Matthew and Andy had gone off in the direction of the toilets, Andy waiting for a few seconds to lapse after Matthew had gone, Jaimini started pretending to be busy at the counter; she was actually keeping an eye on our table, looking out for the signal to tell her to go and get Jan.

We all waited with bated breath for the return of Andy. She came out looking perfectly calm and gave us an extremely subtle thumbs-up sign. We then sat like a load of nervous wrecks until Matthew came out of the loo. This part was the nail-biting bit because if another customer beat Barry to the loo, the whole plan could have been ruined. And with our track record for successful plans, this seemed quite a possibility.

Matthew duly emerged from the loo, and we all breathed out before tensing up again in anticipation of the next part of the plan. We tried not to watch too obviously as Matthew went up to Barry and leaned over to whisper to him. Then once again we let out great sighs of relief as Barry immediately got up, grinning madly and nudging his friends at the same time, before strolling out to the loos.

Andy followed softly behind him, and the moment he was through the door to the ladies', (which he of course thought was the men's) she whipped off the stickers and stole back to her place, moving as silently and rapidly as only Andy can.

That was my cue to nod at Jaimini, who was able to grab Jan with perfect timing, as Jan played right into our hands by coming out of the kitchen at that very second. We couldn't hear what Jaimini said to Jan, but we knew very well what it would be.

She would have said, "Some stupid boy has just gone into the ladies' loo, Jan."

We saw Jan's lips tighten and her expression harden into an "I-won't-stand-for-any-adolescent-pranks-in-*my*-café" expression.

Two seconds later Jan was standing with her hands on her hips outside the loos as a rather hot-and-bothered-looking Barry came out of the ladies', to find himself face to face with the furious café manageress.

Our two tables had ring-side seats for this, because Jaimini had followed Jan through the door to the loos and very thoughtfully left it wide open!

Chapter 9

"Are you blind or something?" Jan shot at Barry, her temper flaring. She jabbed a finger at the original sign on the door from which Barry had just emerged.

He looked at it incredulously and started to try and justify himself.

"But…"

Jan seized his arm and dragged him inside. At this point Matthew and I went and stood in the little passage while Jaimini shut the door to the café, but obligingly held open the door to the ladies' so Matthew and I could watch the scene inside. Jan had completely flipped, so she didn't appear to notice Matthew and me standing there.

Once before, ages ago, Jan had caught a boy emerging from the ladies' loo, and he'd been in there especially to write a message on the door for one of the girls, so that was why Jan was so quick to investigate why Barry had gone into the ladies' in the first place.

The whole thing was working just as I had planned. Jan was reading the message on the door, and looking extremely thunderous.

"So it was *you*, was it?" she practically spat at Barry. Matthew and I knew that she meant the reference to stopping me from winning, but of course Barry hadn't yet seen the words on the inside of the loo door.

"I don't know what you're talking about," he said, holding his palms up as if to show his innocence.

"Fen is my niece, you know," Jan went on.

"So what?" Barry asked, looking slightly uneasy at the sound of my name.

"You may well look embarrassed," Jan said. She then dragged him into the loo to "survey his handiwork" as she put it, then yanked him out again.

"I never wrote that," Barry said crossly.

"If you expect me to believe that, you must think I was born yesterday," Jan retorted. "I shall report you to your headmaster, young man."

At this point Matthew and I slipped back into the café. Neither Jan nor Barry had noticed us there. Jaimini also went back to work.

A moment later Jan came out, stormed into the kitchen and reappeared almost immediately with a scouring pad and some kitchen cleaner. She was obviously making Barry clean the message off.

The two of them emerged together about two minutes later and Jan looked much calmer. She resumed her work, smiling at her customers as though nothing had happened at all. Barry, on the other hand, had obviously had time to do a bit of thinking. He came straight up to our two tables, because two of his three friends had gone and the third one was sitting with Matthew at his table.

"What you sitting with him for?" he asked the friend, who was called Luke. Luke grinned at Barry.

"I've been hearing about your bit of bother," Luke answered, still grinning.

Barry turned to me and glared. "It was you, wasn't it?"

I gave him an over-the-top innocent look. "I don't know what you're talking about."

"Well, it was *you* then, wasn't it?" said Barry, flinging his mounting venom at Matthew. "Or *you*!" He stabbed at Andrea.

We all adopted the same innocent expression which was really getting to Barry.

"She's going to report me," Barry went on, jerking his head vaguely in the direction of the kitchen. "You've got to stop her," he ordered me aggressively. "It isn't fair."

"I think it's perfectly fair," Tash said, bravely. "After all, we all know you did it, don't we?"

"Huh! She can't prove it. It's rubbed off now. No one can prove it." Barry was getting back to his old cocky self.

Luke laughed.

"What are you laughing at?" Barry demanded.

"You. You're mad if you think the Head won't believe a manageress of *The Café*."

Barry was being thoroughly humiliated. Even his friends seemed to have deserted him: two of them, literally, and the third one had apparently lost interest in being friends with a loser.

"But it wasn't even me who wrote that stuff in the loo," he protested in a whiny voice, two red spots appearing high on his cheeks. "It was one of you lot. You're all in it together."

"Yes, you're right, we are," I said, standing up and facing Barry squarely. I looked him right in the eyes and said pointedly, "But you can't prove it. No one can prove it."

There was a wonderful silence, a glorious moment of triumph, which I savoured to the full. The others were all smiling, and as Barry looked from one face to the next he knew he was beaten.

His mouth set firmly, he turned abruptly and was about to storm out, but he changed his mind and we watched the aggression seeping out of him.

"Can't you persuade her not to say anything," he asked me, shuffling from foot to foot. "I didn't know you were going to get stuck in the forest, honest. I just wanted to stop you winning, you know, to pay you back for mucking Matthew about."

"I could persuade her if I wanted to," I said, carefully.

"Yeah, go on. Do us a favour."

"Just remember, Barry, I know the truth, and so does my aunt Jan. If I *do* persuade her not to say anything, it'll be on two conditions."

"Yeah? What?" he asked, eagerly.

"One, that you stop being such a bully to everyone all the time."

"I'm not a... Yeah, OK."

"And two, that you don't even think about laying the blame on Matthew for what you did at the cross-country."

"I wasn't going to."

He turned to go, all jaunty again, probably thinking he'd got off very lightly.

"Because," I warned him in a low voice, "if I ever hear that you're not sticking to my conditions, I'll have to persuade my aunt to go and speak to your head."

"Yeah, OK," he mumbled. "Coming, Luke?"

"Nah."

"See ya, then."

And off he went. It was all we could do not to break into a big cheer when he'd gone. Instead we congratulated each other, and then had another round of congratulations when Jaimini came over. Peta, meanwhile, had fallen asleep in Tash's lap and slept soundly through everything.

"She weighs a ton. I'm going to get going, I think," Tash said.

But she changed her mind immediately because through the door came Mum with Rachel and Emmy!

"I thought I'd find you lot here," Mum said, just as though she was always popping into the café at this time of day.

"What are you doing here, Mum?" I asked, slightly anxiously. Her answer was another question.

"Is Jan about?"

"She must be in the kitchen," said Tash, trying to twist round, despite the heavy weight on her lap.

Without further ado Mum zipped off into the kitchen, leaving Rachel and Emmy standing at our table.

"Sit here if you want," said Andrea to Rachel. "I've got to go."

"So have we, Matthew," Carly said, looking at her watch and becoming agitated. "Mum'll be going spare."

Matthew stood up. "See you tomorrow, then."

"Tomorrow?" asked Luce.

"The cross-country," I quickly reminded her.

"Oh, yes, we'll all be there to support Fen and Andy. See you tomorrow."

Luke went with the others too, and the door had no sooner shut behind them than Mum and Jan emerged from the kitchen together. Jan was holding something. It looked familiar. She and Mum sat down at the places that Matthew and the others had just left.

"It seems you *were* going to speak to me last Sunday after all," said Jan, looking at me properly for the first time for ages.

I just nodded and swallowed.

"I didn't believe you. It all sounded too glib to be true. That was what was upsetting me more than the fact that you deceived your mum and me in the first place. If I really think about it, and think back to when I was your age, I can just about bring myself to understand why you did it, Fen. You'd had a great idea and you couldn't bear to see it all fall through. The bit I couldn't handle was the way you seemed to be coolly getting yourself off the hook by saying you were going to confess everything to me the following day."

"But I *was*…"

"Yes, I know that now."

"How?"

She held something up. It was Andy's card with the picture of the fat, furry, winking rabbit on the front.

"I was vacuuming in your room," explained Mum, "and I found it. Because it was open on your shelf, I couldn't resist reading what it said."

Jan read Andy's card out loud.

Bad luck about the cross-country. We'll get even somehow. Have a great evening – your last one. Hope you're feeling brave about tomorrow. Phone me when you've talked to Jan.

Loads of love

Andy.

Jan let the card drop into her lap, and leant forward to give me a hug. "Sorry pet, I should have believed you."

"It's OK."

"I'm abandoning the Wednesday evenings altogether," she went on. "It's an awful lot of hassle, and not very reliable custom. The magic evening was a success though, so maybe once every few months we'll have a special event like that."

"I bet Mum'd love to help," offered Tash.

"Brilliant," Jan said immediately.

I was pretty speechless during all this. Speechless but very happy. Things had really taken a turn for the better. Mum was smiling her special smile at me.

"Come on, let's get back," she said.

We all agreed it was time to go, and as Tash was putting the sleeping Peta into her buggy, I heard Luce say in a very unsubtle whisper to Andy, "Great card, Andy. And Fen's certainly got even with Barry, hasn't she?"

Andy shushed Luce, but it was too late. Jan had heard her. Let's face it, we'd *all* heard her.

We watched Jan frown, then turn her head towards the door to the loos as though she was trying to work something out. Then she slowly pointed towards the loos. "You mean…" she began, as her hand dropped.

Oh, well done, Luce, I thought sarcastically, feeling my spirits beginning to take a tumble. I tensed up and braced myself for Jan's outburst about mindless vandalism and time wasting. But miraculously, it didn't come. Instead, her face creased up and she clutched hold of Leah, who happened to be standing closest to her, and went completely weak with laughter.

Mum regarded her sister for a moment with a bemused expression on her face, then turned to us lot. "I always knew she was mad, of course," she said. "What *are* you laughing about, Jan?"

"Your daughter's mind," she spluttered. Then seeing Mum look even more puzzled, said, "Go on, Fen, get off home, and tell your Mum what you lot have been up to for the last half hour. And at some point you can tell me how you got that dreadful boy to go into the wrong loo!"

With that we all broke up and went home. Mum didn't find my story quite as funny as Jan had done, but then Mum hadn't been the one to tear Barry off a strip for something he hadn't done, had she!

Not long after we got home, Dad came back, and Rachel got me to tell him the "revenge" story, as she called it. Dad found it funnier than Mum had done, although Mum seemed to appreciate it more the second time.

Then I went outside to see Bracken. What I saw made my heart stop beating. Poor Bracken was having some kind of horrific fit. I rushed in and grabbed Mum and Dad, yelling at them to hurry up. They peered into Bracken's hutch, and looked at each other in alarm.

"I'll call the vet," Dad said immediately. Mum and I stayed with Bracken. When his fit stopped it was obvious he was really ill. He just seemed to flop out suddenly with his head hanging at an awkward angle.

"We've got to get him straight over there," Dad said a couple of minutes later, as he rushed back out into the garden. Mum got a towel, and I gently scooped Bracken out and wrapped him up. He snuggled close to me and stayed quite still, apart from the tremble that shook his little body the whole time.

I sat in the back of the car with Rachel on one side and Emmy on the other, and Bracken huddled up close to my face so the odd tear fell on his fur. This was like the family outing from hell.

Dad and I went into the vet's surgery with Bracken, leaving Mum, Rachel and Emmy in the waiting room. The vet had remembered Bracken's name from Dad's phone call, and he talked to him in a soothing voice as he very gently and thoroughly examined him.

After a very short time, he turned to me and Dad, and spoke the words that I'd been dreading hearing most of all.

"I'm sorry," he began gravely, "but Bracken is very ill indeed. He's got something called Viral Haemorrhagic Disease, or VHD. It's a fatal virus that has come over to this country relatively recently from China. The fits, the very high temperature, the fact that Bracken is so weak and floppy, the sudden onset of the symptoms – all this points to VHD. When did you say you first noticed the symptoms?"

"Only just before I phoned you," Dad answered.

"Yes, but they might have started earlier," I pointed out in a shaky voice. "Mum said she looked in at him at about four o'clock and he was fine then, but we don't know what happened after that, do we?"

I could hardly speak, the lump in my throat was so big. The vet was nodding slowly, his eyes full of sympathy and understanding.

"That's still quite a fast deterioration, and I really think it would be the kindest thing of all to put him down," he said very gently. "He may not be suffering now, but he will be in a matter of an hour or so, and death won't be more than a few hours after that."

As if to prove the vet's point, Bracken went into another fit. The enormous lump in my throat was unbearable and I couldn't prevent a few more tears sliding down my cheeks. Dad put his arm round me and gripped my shoulder tightly, which of course made my tears really flow.

"You know best, Mr Andrews," he said. "We'll leave you to it, then."

I put my face close to Bracken's and whispered goodbye to him, then Dad and I went back into the waiting room to tell Mum the heartbreaking news. Mum had tears in her eyes, and when I looked at Dad I noticed that even *he* had tears in his eyes. Rachel and Emmy were the only two who felt like talking on the way home.

Later, after my sisters had gone to bed, Mum and Dad and I sat round the kitchen table playing

Trionimo, and comforting each other. Nothing that either of them said did any good, though.

I'll never forget that evening. It was one of the worst of my life.

Chapter 10

The following morning, I opened my eyes, sat up, and thought, "Great! Saturday! No school."

My next thought was, "Saturday! Help! Cross-country!"

And then the horrible remembrance hit me.

Saturday – the day after Friday. No more Bracken.

A great heaviness made me flop back into my pillows. I didn't cry. I think I'd cried my grief out of my system the previous day. I just felt so low, so very low.

Mum and Emmy were already up but Rachel was still in bed. Dad had got up very early and gone to meet someone in connection with work.

The cross-country was scheduled for the morning this time, and Mum was taking me in the car with Rachel and Emmy. We had to be there by nine-thirty so there was a lot of rushing about going on in our house that morning. Not by me, though. I didn't have the will to rush. I walked around miserably.

As soon as we arrived at Lowerden Forest School I went straight off to find Mr Cobb. The very sight of the place made me feel like a nervous wreck. My knees were beginning to turn to jelly.

"You're looking pale, Fen," Mr Cobb greeted me. "There's really nothing to worry about. There are stewards all the way round this time." He grinned and rubbed his hands together. "I'm feeling lucky today, you know. I think we're in with a fighting chance."

None of Mr Cobb's enthusiasm wore off on to me, unfortunately. My spirits lifted a teeny bit when Andy turned up. She had that look in her eyes. She meant business, I could tell.

The year-nine girls were more confident too, because they'd got Andy this week. I was the only one who felt completely down. One of the year nines, called Meggy, put her arm round me.

"Just remember how well you were doing last time, Fen. If that stupid flag hadn't taken you on a wild-goose chase you would have won by a mile!"

"I haven't got much energy today," I said despondently.

Mr Cobb gave us all glucose tablets, and we set

off round the course for Andy's benefit. I shivered as we came to the place where I'd gone the wrong way.

"You'll be fine, Fen," Mr Cobb repeated.

"What's up, Fen?" whispered Andy, shortly after that. "There's something else on your mind, isn't there?"

"B... Bracken," I whispered. "He's ... dead."

"Oh, no! Oh, Fen! How?"

We hung back from the others and I told her the whole story in a nutshell, while trying to keep my emotions under control for all I was worth. I knew if I gave into them and started crying again at this stage, I'd never be able to stop.

"I'm really sorry, Fen," Andy kept saying, looking up at me with big, soulful eyes.

"I keep trying to forget about it, at least while I'm here. Then I can sob to my heart's content, after this is all over."

"Right, good thinking. Let's concentrate, then. Come on."

Andy started jogging to catch up with Mr Cobb and the others. I knew she wouldn't mention Bracken again. She would just be bracing and positive about the race. I was glad I could depend on her to do that. It made me feel a little stronger.

When we got back to the starting field, we saw that Jaimini, Luce, Leah and Tash were all there with their families. And Jan had turned up, too. Jan was in a really excited mood. She said she'd left Becky in charge at the café.

Then I saw Matthew and Barry and a bunch of other boys I didn't recognize. Matthew called out "Hi" and I said "Hi" back. Barry just scowled and I decided not to let him get away with that.

"Hello, Barry," I called out, pointedly.

"Oh, hello, Fen," he called back.

Andy and I gave each other knowing smiles, which Barry couldn't have missed. We'd got him right under the thumb!

A few minutes later, when I was standing on my own doing warm-up exercises, Matthew approached me.

"Don't take the mickey out of Barry, Fen. He's trying really hard, honestly."

"That's good to hear," I replied, without stopping my warm-up exercises. But I was actually really pleased to hear that about Barry.

"And, good luck, Fen," Matthew went on. "Er … will I see you afterwards?"

"I expect so," I replied, still without stopping my exercises.

It wasn't until much later that I realized that this was Matthew asking me out. At the time, though, my mind was too preoccupied to even notice.

Unlike the previous Saturday there was only one race to be run that day, the fourteen-and-under girls race. And yet there were an awful lot more spectators this time.

"I've never seen such a big turn-out," Mr Cobb smiled. "You're famous, Fen. That's what it is, you know," he joked.

Then he suddenly turned serious. "Actually, you *are* quite famous, Fen. Look, the press are here, and they're heading in this direction!"

He was right, unfortunately. I really didn't feel like talking to anyone, let alone the press.

"Fenella Brooks?" asked a tall bearded man, striding up to me.

I nodded.

"Do you mind if we talk to you for a few minutes?" The "we" was presumably because of a man with long hair and a large camera standing just behind the bearded man. I looked at Mr Cobb with pleading eyes.

"I think Fenella's concentrating on preparing for the race at the moment," he said, politely smiling from one man to the other.

"No problem, no problem at all," said the bearded man, holding up his hands to show that he wasn't going to be persistent. "Perhaps afterwards?" he asked me.

"Yes, fine," I said, because I thought it would be rude of me to tell the truth and say, "I don't feel like talking, and I definitely don't want my photograph taken. I'm not in the mood, thank you very much."

I went over to Mum to ask her when Dad was coming.

"He'll do his very best to get here in time," she replied. "The only thing that might delay him is the traffic, but he left very early. I'm sure he'll be here in a minute."

But ten minutes went by and still Dad hadn't arrived, and all the competitors were taking their places on the field.

"Don't forget, run like the wind for the first hundred metres," Mr Cobb reminded us for the millionth time, "then just keep up a steady momentum. The more you stick together in a group, the greater the chance for the team. Good luck, girls!"

I could feel the adrenalin beginning to pump round my body, but I didn't think it would be enough to make me run as fast as I knew I had to run. Maybe if I did fairly well, and Andy won, our team would be all right.

"Think positive!" Andy whispered, from her place beside me in the line. I turned sideways to see the expression on her face. As I had thought, she looked as though she could tackle anything at that moment. She gets herself all psyched up, Andy does. It's incredible the way she does it.

"Stick with me," she added. "I'm going to the front."

She wasn't showing off. She was simply stating a fact. I was full of doubt, nervousness and depression. There was no way I'd be able to keep up with Andy. It was all up to the year-nine girls.

"On your marks, get set…" BANG! went the starting pistol.

The crowd immediately broke into yells of encouragement. Everyone was shouting so loudly it was impossible to hear any individual voices. I ran as fast as I could and with every ounce of energy I had, but I just didn't have what it took.

Andy was sprinting ahead, her elbows pumping backwards and forwards. The distance between us was widening but there was absolutely nothing I could do about it. Even Mr Cobb's voice, yelling at me louder than any other voice, didn't help.

"Go on, Fen," he screamed. "Catch her."

I saw Meggy and Gemma get ahead, and then two of the others were quite near me, so the last two members of our team must have been just behind. Compared to the other competitors we were about halfway, and Andy was way out in the lead – where I'd been the last time, I thought sadly.

We set off through the woods and I managed to catch Andy up very slightly when I heard her voice shouting back to me. Or maybe I hadn't caught her up, maybe she had deliberately slowed down to encourage me.

"Where are you, Fen?" she shouted. "Come on!"

But after my brief spurt I couldn't do any more. I was too tense. And anyway, what was the point? I tried to stop myself thinking along those depressing lines. It was making me even slower than I had been.

"Go on, Fen," Mr Cobb yelled again, and then Mum and Tash's mum were shouting too. "Go on, Fen!"

I knew Andy's mum was standing with Mum too, but they had no need to shout encouragement to Andy. She simply didn't need it. After a bit I heard Jaimini and the others chanting away.

"Go Fen! Go Fen! Go Fen!" over and over at the tops of their voices. But I wasn't going anywhere. It was almost as bad as one of those nightmares where your legs won't work properly.

At the first overtaking point three people passed me, one of our team and two from other schools, and there were several people between me and Andy. My legs felt so heavy.

"Come on, Fen, we need you," came a breathless urge from behind me. It was Jayne, one of the year-nine girls. She was using me as the pacer, and I wasn't going fast enough to stretch her pace and make her go faster. I tried a bit harder but my heart just wasn't in it.

"I'm sorry, I can't," I rasped, feeling my breathing too tight.

Mr Cobb had given up shouting. The spectators and supporters were dotted about all over the place by then. We were about halfway through the course and there were plenty of ways that those watching could take short cuts and get ahead of some of the runners, then give them encouragement at a further point.

I had reached a fairly quiet bit of the course but it didn't worry me at all. There were stewards all over the place. I went past the flag that Barry had turned the other way the last time. This time he was standing beside it.

"Go on, Fen, go for it. Otherwise it won't have been worth rerunning the race," he said.

Matthew had been right. Barry really *had* changed. I smiled a tired smile but didn't answer.

I was just feeling proud of myself for having had a hand in the transformation of Barry, when I heard Tash's voice. She wasn't calling out any of the usual things. In fact, I couldn't make out what on earth she was saying or where her voice was coming from. I listened and waited for it to come again, and after a few seconds, sure enough, it did. Only this time it was a bit louder.

There was still no way I could make out exactly

what she was saying but it sounded like "Your Daggery Scott Track". She repeated it, her voice full of urgency, and I ran a bit harder to get closer to her sooner.

The nearer I got the clearer she became, but I didn't dare believe what I thought she was saying. It couldn't possibly be true. It just couldn't. I began to think I was hearing things. Perhaps I was ill and I was getting delirious. Maybe that was why my legs hadn't been working properly.

And then I was level with her. I saw her rapt smile.

"Your dad's here. He's got Bracken," she repeated.

"Are you sure?" I called back.

But I'd gone past her already – far past. My legs had lost their weakness suddenly. I realized I was approaching Luce. She was grinning like a Cheshire cat.

"Bracken's better! All better! Honestly!"

"Are you sure?" I repeated for the second time, and again I didn't hear her answer because I'd left Luce far behind. My arms were pumping now, hard and fast. I sped past Gemma, Meggie and two others from another school at the next overtaking. And there was Jaimini.

"Have you actually *seen* Bracken?" I yelled, before reaching her.

"Yes, yes! He's cured!" cried Jaimini.

This time I heard her loud and clear. Leah was standing just ten metres further on from Jaimini.

"Go on, Fen!" she screamed. "Andy says 'Hurry up!'"

And that did it. Never before or since have I had that kind of power in my body. I didn't feel as though my body was mine. I was running on air, running, running like the wind, and my heart was singing, "Bracken's alive! Bracken's alive!"

I had overtaken another six people and was ahead of everyone in my own team, except Andy now.

"Come on, Fen!" screamed Mum and Dad from far ahead.

I looked up and saw that Dad was holding a big bundle. I could have cried I was so happy. Pulling together every single last ounce of energy I had, I ran with all my might after Andy. I could see her now.

"Go on, Fen!" yelled a voice behind me. It was Jayne.

She sounded about thirty metres behind me. That meant our team was in with a chance. A *big* chance! In fact, if we took the first three places we'd surely win the competition.

"Do it for Bracken!" came Dad's voice from the finishing point.

I was approaching the funnel, gaining on Andy the whole time. A steward was standing right beside the entrance to the funnel, because that was the place where the final order was decided. As you went into the funnel you went in single file.

Andy's hand was reaching behind to me. I stretched my own hand out and took hers as we entered the funnel.

"Which one's first?" yelled the steward. "You can't go in there together."

"Yes, we can. We're together. Sorry," Andy called with a laugh.

And that's how we stayed, side by side, holding hands right to the end of the funnel, where the finishing judge laughed out loud, and cried, "Well, this has got to be a first! We've never had this before!"

"Thanks for waiting," I gasped to Andy.

"I *didn't* wait. You caught up. What happened? Did you grow a pair of wings?"

"This happened," I said, dragging her with me over to Dad.

"Is this…?" began Andy, eyeing the furry face sticking out from inside a big fluffy towel.

She obviously hadn't dared to finish her sentence in case this wasn't Bracken. After all, she'd never seen Bracken before.

"This is Bracken, yes," I answered, and Dad handed him over.

His little face snuggled into my neck and I

cuddled him as tightly as I could without squashing him, while rocking from side to side.

Mum and Jan were laughing and crying all at once. Emmy was jumping up and down with excitement, and Rachel was leaning into me with her head on my shoulder.

"You were the best, Fen," she whispered.

"That's what I thought," said Dad, brushing away what might have been a tear.

"It's a miracle, Dad. How come Bracken's better? I don't understand."

"When I got back from my work appointment and rushed into the house to grab the camera, the phone was ringing. I nearly didn't answer it because I didn't want to be late for your race. Thank goodness I did, because it was the vet telling me he'd got wonderful news.

"He said that after we'd gone he decided to give Bracken an extremely strong dose of antibiotics, just in case the illness turned out to be a bad case of pneumonia. Apparently a really bad case of pneumonia could possibly be mistaken for that fatal disease he was talking about, although he'd thought the chances of it being pneumonia were almost non-existent. The only reason he decided to try it as a last resort was because he was haunted by the look in your eyes, Fen.

"It was a tough decision for the vet to make, because he then had to wait to see what happened, and if he'd been wrong about the pneumonia, poor Bracken would have had his life unnecessarily prolonged, and would have had to suffer a very painful last few hours.

"He kept his eye on Bracken for the next six hours, because if the symptoms persisted he knew he'd have to put him out of his misery. But apparently the miracle happened, and gradually Bracken stopped having fits, and his temperature dropped very slightly. Apparently, had it been that viral disease – what's it called? – VHD, the symptoms would have got worse and Bracken probably would have been haemorrhaging, too.

"At midnight the vet decided the worst was over, and though Bracken was still ill, it couldn't have been VHD. It was obviously really bad pneumonia.

"I went straight over and collected Bracken and thought about taking him home, but decided that he would be much happier and just as warm cuddled up with me, acting like a big soppy mascot for his owner!"

"You're not big and soppy, are you?" I whispered into Bracken's ear. He blinked at me slowly. "But you *are* my lucky mascot," I added softly.

"There's a man with a beard and a notebook followed by a man with long hair and a camera approaching you, Fen. Now what makes me think they're from the press?" Dad said, smiling at his own wit.

I glanced up, but at the same time I saw Mr Cobb with Meggy, Gemma, Jayne and the others. Andy and I jogged over to them. I was still holding Bracken. I didn't feel quite ready to let him go yet.

Mr Cobb was over the moon.

"Fen, you were sensational!" he declared. "And Andy, what a fantastic performance! In fact, I've never seen anything like the double act you two pulled off!"

The year-nine girls clustered round us and stroked Bracken.

"How did we do?" Andy asked.

"I'll give you one guess," laughed Mr Cobb.

Andy didn't even use up her guess. She looked at me and smiled a very special Andy smile.

"I couldn't have done it without you," I told her happily.

"And we couldn't have done it without you," the year-nine girls told me exuberantly.

By then all the competitors had completed the run, and everyone was assembling around us. The man from the paper and the photographer were trying to get through the tightening crowd of spectators. I felt quite sorry for them, struggling like that.

The Headmaster spoke in a loud, clear,

authoritative voice, which made everyone silent in no time at all.

"Ladies and Gentlemen," he began. "I can say without hesitation that this has been quite the most dramatic race I have ever been privileged to witness…" A happy murmur passed through the spectators, then fizzled away.

Jan caught my eye at that moment and gave me a double thumbs-up sign, then grabbed both of Mum's thumbs and made Mum hold them up beside her own two. I knew exactly what Jan was trying to say. She meant that I'd got four brilliant pieces of luck. I did a mental tot up… One, I'd got Bracken back; two, our team had won the race; three, I'd paid Barry back, and four, the Café Club was back to its good old self.

I grinned and nodded.

"…So a complete departure from normal," the Headmaster was saying. "I'd like the *two* winners –" he stressed the word *two*, which sent a delighted titter running through the crowd – "to come and receive the cup!"

So up we went together.

I was still holding Bracken so Andy took the cup and held it high. In true sporting tradition, she kissed the cup, and at the same time I kissed Bracken, which sent another wave of laughter through the crowd.

Then suddenly we found ourselves being the

very centre of attention as loads of clicks sounded and the odd flash went off. I glanced over at the men from the press. The bearded man was pushing his way determinedly through the crowd.

Eventually he reached my side. The crowd fell silent.

"How do you feel at this very moment?" he asked me.

I didn't hesitate.

"It's like a dream come true," I answered.

"In fact, it *is* a dream come true," Andy and I said at exactly the same moment, as we turned to each other with laughing eyes.

"Get that one, quick!" the journalist said to the photographer. "Come on, Bill, you'll never get a shot as good as that one."

But I noticed the photographer didn't take the picture. He just stood there. Then Andy reached her hand out to stroke Bracken as I looked round for Mum and Dad in the crowd. I saw Mum first and gave her a big smile.

At that moment Bracken popped his head right out of the towel with such vigour that I thought he was going to jump out of my arms altogether. Andy must have had the same thought, because she quickly thrust the big silver cup underneath him as if to save his fall. Everybody laughed because it looked just as though Bracken was sitting in the cup. My eye caught Dad's and he gave me a broad wink.

It was as I was winking back that I saw the flash from the photographer's camera.

"Got it!" said Bill.

Join

Would you and your friends like to know more
about Fen, Tash, Leah, Andy, Jaimini and Luce?

We have produced a special bookmark to
commemorate the launch of the Café Club
series. To get yours free, together with a
special newsletter about Fen and her friends,
their creator, author Ann Bryant, and advance
information about what's coming next in
the series, write (enclosing a self-addressed
label, please) to:

The Café Club
c/o the Publicity Department
Scholastic Children's Books
Commonwealth House
1-19 New Oxford Street
London WC1A 1NU

We look forward to hearing from you!